Guarding Clare

A Ransom Mayes Novel

Mary M. Bauer

Cover art: CURAphotography/Shutterstock.com
Author photograph: Shoe Button Photography by Jessica Gilliland
Cover design and page layout: coversbykaren.com

ISBN 978-0-9990475-2-1

Reader praise for GUARDING CLARE
This book was previously published as Step One

"I love this book! I have it all dog-eared, high-lighted, and tear-stained. Beautiful story. I feel like I am Clare!"

"I couldn't put this book down, it was so good. I have my clients read this book to understand how their thoughts affect their lives."

"THANK YOU for this open and Divinely-inspired communication."

"The book was a life changer."

"I loved this book! Could not put it down. Many insights that click with life. Bought on Audible so I can listen to it over and over."

"I didn't want it to end! Keeps your interest until the very last word!"

"I read this book a few times and got something new out of it every time. A fast, easy read with life-changing info."

"This is a wonderful story that explains energy, the magic within each of us, and our connection to Spirit. A fantastic read!"

"This insightful and intriguing story leads readers to explore their own connection with guardians/angels as well as their purpose in life and in the universe. An engaging read!"

"Wonderful, informative, and intriguing read! Loved the characters. This book answers questions I've had in an easy way that I can understand. Great book."

"I'm delighted I found this book on a friend's reading list. Thank you Mary for this spiritual adventure filled with helpful reminders, tips, and exercises for growing spiritually."

Acknowledgments

Of the many who gave me help, I am deeply grateful to these insightful, loving, fun beings—aka: my early manuscript readers. This book would not be the message it is without them: Mary Bates, Nancy Bauer, Robert Bauer, Lori Beskau, Don Briggs, Jackie Churchill, Connie Cockriel Collison, Margie Collett, Renee Keene, Ruth Luebker, Shelly Opelt, Lorraine Painter, Jennifer Raskob Kranz, Dawn Schubert, Sarah Stinson, Lynda Thibado.

For unfailing good advice—always: Meredith Rutter.

For unconditional love and the space to be me—my family and friends.

For the story and wisdom—Source and its legion of messengers. #ransomfan!

Dedication

For you sparkly creators who listen to your hearts.

Chapter One

RANSOM Mayes fought a bitter north wind as he rode his bicycle up a steep, icy hill. His breathing came in raspy white bursts, and his boot-clad feet frequently slipped off the pedals, costing time he didn't have.

To the casual observer, Ransom could pass as a college student, anxious for a warm bed after a shift waiting tables at one of the nearby pubs. Dressed in layers designed to keep out the cold, the hooded parka didn't hide his streaked blond hair, or freakish eyes so green they were the first thing people noticed about him.

Ransom glanced over his shoulder. The street was empty, as had been the case whenever he checked, yet he couldn't shake the feeling of being followed. A crazy thought since no one knew he existed.

Dipping his head into the wind, Ransom put his mind back on the task at hand. He knew what was at stake. A tardy minute meant a premature death for someone who wasn't prepared. He couldn't let that happen. Would *not* let that happen. He saved lives. He would save this one, too.

The street crested, and Ransom pumped the bicycle faster. A loud crack overhead dropped a large, ice-covered tree branch in his path. Skidding left, he avoided brittle limbs as they shattered on the frozen street, but overcompensated by leaning too far right. His boot caught on the ice and he spun around landing hard, face down, sprawled across the pavement. A bloody gash on his chin went unnoticed as he righted the bike and got back on, thankful it hadn't been damaged.

Pedaling for all he was worth, the shrill wind whistled in his ears and whipped his face raw. Hugging low in the seat, Ransom tightened his grip on the handlebars, no longer able to feel his fingertips. He took a sharp corner cutting through a crowded nightclub parking lot, weaving his way between cars.

A door to the club opened, flooding the night with a rectangle of yellow light and the pulsing sound of a bass guitar. For a moment, Ransom was drawn to the inviting warmth inside. What he wouldn't give for a steaming mug of whiskey-laced coffee and the chance to thaw his frozen feet.

Such comforting thoughts. They were his last. From the corner of his eye he saw red taillights an instant before the car's rear bumper rammed him.

d

Clare Davis checked her coat at the door and peered across the packed, dimly lit nightclub taking stock of her surroundings. The space had an upscale artsy vibe with its funky paintings and exposed brick walls. Smiling, beautiful people sat in plush velvet chairs around low tables sipping imported liquors and the club's signature drinks.

Clare pulled a self-conscious hand through her hair knowing she was grossly underdressed in leggings and a long, bulky sweater—items she'd hastily gathered from her bedroom floor. Most patrons dismissed her with less than a glance.

Not that she cared what anyone thought. Clare was on a mission. Forty minutes earlier she'd slept with her boyfriend Keith Paulson, a handsome tax attorney she'd been dating for six months. He was charming and attentive, but it bothered her that he wouldn't stay the night no matter how much she begged. His excuse? He was a horrible sleeper, restless and wild. How could he live with himself if he hurt her?

Fair enough, Clare had thought, but it didn't explain why he wouldn't take her anywhere. Six months of Chinese takeout and pizza delivery gets a gal wondering what's wrong with this picture. Was he ashamed of her? At age twenty-eight she wasn't model perfect, not that she had ever been, but she didn't think herself too hideous to take to a movie.

So tonight, after Keith left her bed, Clare got in her car and trailed him. As she searched the crowd, part of her felt like a criminal. Where was her trust? But the uncertain side needed answers, especially after catching him glance at the clock while they made love. A large chunk of her world got shaky when she saw him enter the club.

Shouldering her purse, Clare threaded her way to the bar and tried to suppress the sinking feeling in her gut. *Don't jump to conclusions*, she reminded herself. *He's probably doing someone's taxes.*

Customers stood two deep waiting for drinks. The bar's blue under lighting cast them in ghostly elegance. Clare scanned the lineup. No Keith. At six foot three inches tall with linebacker shoulders, she didn't imagine he'd be too hard to find. The problem was what to say when she found him? She'd left her apartment in a hurry and hadn't thought things through. Maybe she could tell him she was meeting a friend.

She shook her head. No good. Lying wasn't her strong suit. She'd turn red-faced with guilt, and he'd see right through her. She couldn't even call in to work if she wasn't sick.

She had to tell Keith the truth. Not that telling the truth had worked in her favor with her last boyfriend. A pang of regret tugged at her heart. Shaking off the dark thought, she squared her shoulders. Keith was different, and hopefully—fingers crossed—he'd view her being at the club as testament to how much she cared for him.

She let out a groan. Who was she kidding? She knew how much he valued his privacy. Was she willing to destroy everything they had together for her silly insecurities?

An anxious, gnawing sensation wormed its way from her belly to her throat. Rapidly, everything became clear. She loved Keith and he loved her. Whatever reason he had for being at the club was none of her business, and she needed to leave *now*. Spying on him was a bad idea.

The back exit was a short distance from the stage. Clare pushed her way through the bystanders toward the door, praying she wouldn't run into Keith. Halfway there, she was struck in her tracks by the sight of her boyfriend on the dance floor with an attractive woman. Plastered together, they swayed to the music, barely moving, gazing soulfully into one another's eyes. The woman's hair fell in shimmering gold down her back, and her leather skirt was shorter and tighter and considerably more expensive than anything in Clare's closet.

She watched as Keith's lips slowly slid over the blonde's slender neck, pressing tender kisses at the sensitive nape—the spot he knew made Clare shiver with need for him. Wrapped in the moment, Clare knew neither had a clue she was less than ten feet away staring in horrified disbelief.

People and noise blurred. Clare felt like she was going to be sick, but she couldn't turn away. The woman tipped her face to Keith's, and he kissed her with a passionate urgency that made Clare's face flame with humiliation. Obviously, neither gave a flying fig they were in the middle of a packed dance floor making out like horny teenagers in front of everyone. In front of *her*.

Something inside Clare snapped. With hands fisted at her sides, she marched over to Keith and sharply tapped his shoulder. Turning his lustful gaze on her, he was all lipstick-smeared smiles until his sex-hazed brain came into focus. His eyes went wide. "Clare?"

Rage climbed in a hot flush up Clare's neck. The urge to slap that perfect face was fierce. She said, "Thought you had an early morning client meeting. Since when does tax research involve fifty ways to jam your tongue down someone's throat?"

Puzzled, the blonde in Keith's arms arched her brows at him. "Babe? Who is this?" she asked.

Clare's eyes narrowed. *Yes, Keith, tell Miss Leather Skirt who I am.*

Keith's face turned ashen as he looked from Clare to the woman. A fake laugh gurgled from his throat ending in a coughing fit. The thought he might choke cheered Clare some. How dare he mess around on her with this woman!

Recovering, Keith smiled sweetly at the blonde, planting a reassuring kiss to her palm. "She's no one. A secretary from the firm."

Clare couldn't believe her ears. What a liar! She clenched her teeth. "I am *not* a secretary. Keith, tell this woman who I am."

He stared at Clare as if she were demented. "Oh. Right. *Executive assistant.*"

Keith rolled his eyes at the blonde as if to say "see what I have to put up with," and hustled her off the dance floor away from Clare.

Couples swirled around Clare as she watched Keith guide the woman out of earshot, his hand possessively at the small of her back. This intimate gesture felt even more devastating than the make-out session she'd witnessed. Jealousy pricked Clare's heart. Why was he treating her like this? Who was this woman?

Her boyfriend and the blonde stood together a moment talking; the woman's disapproving eyes on Clare the entire time. Keith pulled his wallet from a back pocket and when he handed it to her, Clare caught a glint of light off her third finger. The woman was wearing a wedding ring! *Three karats of he's-totally-married-you-idiot.* The air left her lungs in one gasp. How could she not have known?

Keith bent to give the woman a kiss, but she pulled away and set off for the bar with her nose in the air. Men's heads swiveled in her wake. Keith watched her settle in before turning cold eyes on Clare. A shiver went through her. No one had ever looked at her with such hate.

Suddenly the club noise was unbearable, the walls too close, the lights too bright. Dark spots floated in front of Clare's face and panic erupted in her chest. She was minutes away from a full-blown migraine.

She tried to pull herself together, but people were staring. A couple danced close to her and smirked, their silent message told her she was too pathetic for words. Clare turned from them, the neon exit sign straight ahead. As she stumbled toward the door, Keith caught her roughly by the elbow and hissed in her ear. "We need to talk."

Shoving the door open, Keith yanked her with him into the freezing cold of a lighted alley, a space designated for smokers. But tonight there were no smokers. The brutal windchill kept them away.

Keith released her and spun on his heels, his handsome features hard with contempt. "What the hell are you doing here?"

Withering under his harsh stare, Clare silently cursed herself for her weakness. She was not the one at fault here. He was. She lifted her chin. "I followed you."

"You *followed* me." He shook his head. "Not cool."

"Is she your wife?"

His nostrils flared. "That's not your concern."

"Not my *concern*? I fell in love with you, you jerk. You made me think our relationship meant something."

Angry tears sprung from her eyes and Keith's glare softened. Good. Let him see the pain he's caused.

He tenderly thumbed a tear from her face. "We do have something. I don't want to lose you."

She slapped his hand away. "You disgust me."

He snorted, cruelness in his expression an hour earlier Clare wouldn't have thought possible. Eyeing her as if she were a rabid dog, he took a step back and adjusted his tie. "It didn't have to be like this. We had a good thing."

"*You* had a good thing. You told me I was special."

His voice dropped. "Oh honey, you are special. No one gives head like you do."

With a quick tug on his shirt cuffs, Keith strolled through the door without looking back. Clare clasped a hand over her heart. She couldn't believe how much his meanness hurt. The pain was unbearable. Maybe she'd luck out and have a heart attack.

The swiftness of the thought stunned her, and yet boosted her spirits. A year of therapy and there it was—the truth. She wanted to die. There were a thousand reasons to shut her eyes and not wake. Why keep struggling? In fact, the more she thought about dying the more peaceful she felt.

The door banged open, caught by the wind. A scrawny guy in a rumpled suit stepped into the bitter cold, a cigarette pressed between thin lips. He gave her a quick nod before putting his shoulder to the wind, wasting no time lighting up.

Clare shivered, her knees weakening as adrenaline waned. Dying was one thing. But it was unthinkable to die in front of a guy hacking out a lung in an alley where her boyfriend dumped her. No, she would be warm at least. And she would be wearing something other than wretched black leggings. She'd have to forget about her coat. No way could she go back inside and risk running into Keith and *that woman*.

Walking briskly through the alley toward her car in the lot, Clare's purse bounced at her hip. The muffled music from inside the club provided a beat for her silent mantra:

I want to die.

I want to die.

I want to die.

Clare spotted her Camry beneath a brightly lit security lamp. An hour ago she cared about her safety. How freeing not to give a rat's ass about that now.

Numb fingers fumbled in her purse for keys. Unlocking the door, she crawled inside huddling behind the steering wheel. Getting the key into the ignition took patience, her shaking hands nearly uncontrollable. Thankfully, the engine turned right over and she shifted into reverse with one thought in mind: God, help me die.

A loud thud from behind her made Clare stomp on the brake. Her eyes flew to the rearview mirror, certain she'd backed into another car. Not seeing anything, she got out to check. She'd noticed broken glass on the ground earlier. A flat tire would be perfect for this horrible night.

The tires on the driver's side looked good. As she approached the rear, her heart lodged in her throat. On the ground was a young man in a crumpled heap, a bicycle next to him. He wasn't moving. A dark streak on his chin looked like it might be blood.

Frantic, Clare ran for the club and rushed the first people she saw—a young couple pulling on coats. "Help! A man in the parking lot is hurt!"

The couple glanced at each other and quick understanding passed between them. Handing her his cellphone, the man said to Clare, "My wife will call an ambulance. I'm a paramedic. Show me where he is."

Darting from the nightclub, Clare raced to her car with the paramedic a step behind. Kneeling beside the young man, he felt for a pulse at the neck while white clouds spewed from the Camry's exhaust.

"Shut off your car," the paramedic told her.

Obeying, Clare killed the engine. When she returned, he was gently rolling the man onto his back. Hugging her arms, Clare stood off to the side, her teeth chattering. "I-I was backing out and I heard a noise. I got out to look… oh, God." Tears pricked her eyes. She swallowed hard. "Will he be all right?"

Glancing up at Clare, the paramedic's expression was serious. "I'll do what I can. Do you know him?"

"No." She shook her head. "He looks so young."

The paramedic listened close to the man's mouth, brows drawn in concentration. Clare saw white breath coming from the paramedic, but nothing from the man lying on the ground. Everything about him was still. Too still. Fear seized her. She had to look away to keep from screaming.

The paramedic's wife approached, followed by a panting, heavyset man. "An ambulance is twenty minutes away," she told him.

He shook his head. "Too long. I can't get a pulse. We need to move him inside where it's warm and start CPR."

"I'm the club manager," the heavyset man said to the paramedic. "Anything I can do to help?"

"Can you lift?"

"Yes. Where do you want me?"

"Opposite me. We'll each take a side." The paramedic looked at his wife. "Can you hold his head?"

She nodded and knelt at the man's head.

The paramedic turned to Clare and she shrank back, bile rising. She couldn't stop shaking. "H-he's d-dead, isn't he? I know he's dead."

Shrugging out of his jacket, the paramedic helped Clare into it. "Better?" he asked.

Her whole body shook, but the warmth of his jacket did make her feel better.

"What's your name?" he asked.

"C-Clare."

The paramedic placed a firm hand on her shoulder, his calm eyes held hers. His tone was straightforward as he explained what he wanted to do. "Clare, we're going to move this man indoors so I can help him. You hold his feet, and we'll do the rest."

Marshalling what courage she could, Clare let him lead her to the man's feet. She studied the black treads on his boots, anything to keep from thinking about what she was doing.

Taking position near the man's chest, the paramedic gave instructions. "On the count of three, we'll lift." He looked around the group. "One. Two. Three."

Without warning, the young man's eyes flew open. Sucking in a loud, gasping breath, he bolted upright into a sitting position. Clare screamed, jerking away, and so did the paramedic's wife. The manager fell onto his backside clutching his chest. "Christ. What the hell?"

Eyes wide, the paramedic grabbed the young man's arm. "Whoa, there. Easy, buddy."

The young man rolled his neck, stretching, and moved his jaw a couple times. He blinked at the people circling him. "What's going on?"

"You were in an accident," the paramedic said. "The ambulance is on the way. Why don't you lie down?"

"Why? I feel pretty good. Jaw's kind of sore is all."

Looking around, he spotted his bicycle. Before the

paramedic could stop him, the young man was on his feet and straddling the bike. About to push off, the paramedic stepped in front of him and held onto the handlebars. "Let me take you to the hospital. You weren't breathing. You didn't have a pulse. Technically, you were dead."

The young man grinned warmly at the paramedic, his clear green eyes sparkled. "I'm okay, I promise. You can let go."

Reluctantly, the paramedic moved back. "Your life."

Along with the others, Clare watched the young man ride away, barely able to believe her remarkable luck. The guy was alive! Not only was he alive, but healthy enough to ride his bike. He hadn't even asked for her address or her insurance information or anything. She wanted to dance with relief, until she remembered her death wish. A shudder went through her. This night could have ended so differently.

The young man turned onto the street, and gave them a wave. Before disappearing into the night, he called from over his shoulder. "See you later, Clare."

At his words, her stomach lurched. How did he know her name?

Chapter Two

THE baggage claim area of the Minneapolis-St. Paul International airport was a hive of activity. Several planeloads of people had converged around the carousels waiting for their luggage to appear.

Dressed in a sweatshirt and faded jeans, Ransom Mayes leaned against a cement pillar with his parka folded over an arm. He had his eye on a pair of men who had flown in from Las Vegas. In his line of work, he'd run into these types before—big and muscular with thick necks and thicker skulls. Ransom had no doubt they could tenderize a side of beef with their bare hands.

The men wore dark slacks and jackets, and each towed a black carry-on suitcase. Their Italian leather shoes would prove worthless against the drifting snow outside. The younger was white haired and fair. His partner had olive skin, a trimmed beard, and steely black eyes. Ransom had watched them step off the escalator, the bearded man out front. He was likely the one in charge.

The pair planted themselves at the first carousel where the luggage came off the chute. A menacing glare from the white-haired man ensured no one stood within an arm's length of them.

Ransom had been warned these men would come and he knew what they wanted—Clare. His jaw clenched. She had no idea the danger surrounding her, or the enormous power she possessed within her to stop it. In simplest terms, Clare Davis was born to save the world, but she didn't remember this fact. His job was to help her remember while keeping her safe. And by God, that's what he'd do.

A flirtatious giggle interrupted his thoughts and Ransom rolled his eyes skyward. Three women, roughly his age, stood a short distance from him. They had been trying to get his attention for the past fifteen minutes by making eyes at him and fawning over his looks. Accustomed to this type of unsolicited interest, Ransom ignored them and hoped they'd shove off. *It's just a face*, he muttered under his breath.

The women did not give up easily. From the corner of his eye, Ransom saw the bravest of the trio fluff her hair and smooth her sweater, prepping to make her move. An annoyed sigh escaped his lips when she strutted toward him.

He had no time for this foolishness. Fortunately, he'd learned a thing or two about repelling women. Picking his nose, Ransom removed a booger and flicked it off his finger.

The woman, who had been so intent on making his acquaintance, halted mid-strut, mouth open, nose wrinkled with disgust. Skirting back to her friends, the three quickly walked away, faces scrunched in revulsion. Ransom allowed himself a small grin of satisfaction.

A loud buzzer sounded and the carousel spun to life. The passengers wedged closer, jockeying for positions. Identical black handgun cases slid onto the belt. The hair rose on the back of Ransom's neck when the men grabbed them. The situation was much worse than he thought.

Having gotten their luggage, they muscled through the crowd, ignoring protests from the people they shouldered out of their way. Ransom ducked in with a group of rowdy Gopher hockey fans and followed the men to a car rental company. Ransom reasoned it would be helpful to know the type of vehicle his enemy drove. Grabbing a brochure from the kiosk, he pretended to read it as he stepped in line.

Slowly, the line shuffled forward. The woman in front of him hefted a large, canvas tote over her shoulder and nudged the boy at her side to move with her. Jacket zipped to his chin, the child looked to be around four years old. The woman brushed back his matted hair, concern on her face. "Sweetie, you're sweating."

Stooping, she unzipped the boy's jacket. He let out a low, steady hum, eyes staring at an undetermined point on the floor in front of him. With effort, she managed to free an arm before the boy's humming turned high-pitched. Rocking back and forth, he frantically rubbed a small toy car over his cheeks, making them red.

The woman ignored the humming and dug in her tote, producing a worn scrap of blue cloth. Gently, she tried to swap the car in the boy's hand for the cloth. The boy turned rigid and clutched the car tighter, making loud grunting noises.

People around them stared. Ransom glanced at the men who were at the counter talking with the clerk. So far this woman and boy hadn't drawn their attention. If these men suspected he was Clare's guardian, they would head straight for her.

Ransom strained to listen, trying to determine what type of vehicle they were leasing. Something black. An SUV? He couldn't be positive with all the racket the boy was making. Something had to be done about the kid.

Ransom leaned forward and gave the woman his most encouraging smile. "Need help?"

The woman stiffened, deep mistrust in her expression. Ransom noted the dark circles underneath her eyes she had tried to conceal with makeup. "Thanks. We'll manage," she said, and held out a hand to the boy. "Sweetheart, let Mommy have the car."

Despite her calm, reassuring tone, the boy dug harder into his face, leaving tracks of angry welts. Desperate tears welled in her eyes. "Baby, you're hurting yourself. Here's your softy."

When she held the scrap of cloth to his cheek, he screamed bloody murder as if he'd been doused with scalding water.

People gaped in alarm. The white-haired man gave the boy an irritated glance, and turned back to the clerk. The bearded man was even less interested, but his attention lingered when he caught Ransom's eye.

Ransom looked at the floor, and an icy chill seeped into his bones as he felt those black eyes rake him. This man was capable of great cruelty. For Clare's sake, he dropped to one knee pretending to tie his shoelace. It was imperative he look weak and nonthreatening, a harmless nobody who happened to be waiting in line behind a kid with a scream loud enough to break eardrums.

When Ransom sensed the man's curiosity fade, he ventured a look in his direction. Both men were busy signing papers.

Relieved, Ransom concentrated on what to do to help the boy. Closing his eyes a moment, a thought came to him. He took a few deep breaths before blowing softly on the back of the boy's neck. The screaming stopped as the child calmed, resuming the less aggravating hum. Everyone breathed a collective sigh.

The mother was astonished. "How did you do that?"

He shrugged. "I'm good with kids."

"You must be. It takes hours to settle him when he gets like this."

"Happy to help," he said.

Happier still, he could now hear the conversation at the counter. The car lease was for a black Ford Expedition.

Throwing on his coat, Ransom hustled to the exit in time to board the light rail train. A pretty redhead eyed him and scooted over so he could sit in the seat beside her. As he contemplated his next move, the redhead cleared her throat and said, "From the look of that frown, I'd hate to be the person you're thinking about."

Ransom turned toward her and she gave him a knowing smile. "Let me guess. Girlfriend problems?"

He held her gaze. She was a beauty. Deep, violet eyes. Full lips. A few freckles on her nose made her look approachable. "What makes you think I'm having girlfriend problems?"

Staring at his face, her eyes glinted with amusement. "Wishful thinking, I suppose. Was I right?"

Ransom played along. "And if you were?"

She studied him as if she were making a monumental decision, and handed him a business card from her purse. She said, "I'm not usually so forward, but this is my number if you'd like to call me."

Ransom fingered the raised lettering. Over the years he'd taken cards from many women. Single, married, it didn't matter. All wanted his company, including a few men. People were unconsciously drawn to his energy and he knew it. There were no rules against his having fun as long as it didn't interfere with his work.

The woman's eyes searched his with hopeful longing and he was mightily tempted, but he'd have to pass. It wouldn't be right. Although not a mind reader, Ransom did possess unique talents. One of those talents allowed him to know specific things about people. What he knew about this lovely creature was she had given her heart to another. As much as it pained him, he handed back her card. Her face fell.

"Don't get me wrong," he said. "I'm already kicking myself. A guy would have to be a complete bonehead to not want to call you."

"You do have a girl, then?"

He shifted in his seat. "Don't you? A boyfriend, I mean? Pretty girl like you must have someone?"

His question hung in the air a beat, until the truth of it sunk in and her eyes went wide. Cheeks flaming with embarrassment, she clapped her hands over her face. If it were possible, she was even more breathtaking. "What you must think," she frowned, disgusted with herself. "I don't know what's come over me."

Ransom felt sympathetic toward her. She wasn't to blame for her actions. Most people found his high energy irresistible, if not addicting, until they learned for themselves how to raise their own energy.

The train slowed, with his destination fast approaching. The last thing Ransom wanted was to leave her with feelings of guilt. Nothing good came from it. This, he knew well.

Ransom bumped shoulders with her. "Hey, you. I'd like to tell you how flattered I am and how much you made my day, but I feel kind of silly talking to your hands."

She uncovered her face, and gave him a weak smile. "What a dope, huh?"

"Hell, no. I'm gorgeous. I'd ask me out too if I wasn't busy carrying around my big head."

Her laugh was rich and throaty, and holy Jesus, if he didn't like that about her, too.

As the train pulled into the station, Ransom stood and said his good-byes. When the doors opened, he stepped onto the platform. It was time to put his mind on the business at hand. He had a plan, but for it to work he needed Clare's trust. Until last night, she hadn't known he existed. Maybe he should have stepped into her life sooner? If he had, there might be a rapport between them.

Ransom dismissed the thought. Rarely did he allow his charges to see his face. He found he was more effective behind the scenes where there was a lot less drama to deal with. Unfortunately, the situation had degraded to the point where stealth was a foolhardy luxury.

His jaw tightened as he thought of the charge he lost. The pain of his failure was as raw as the day it happened. Pulling himself to his full six-foot height, he made a promise to himself. He would *not* lose this one no matter what it cost him. Clare Davis might not like it, but he was about to become her new best buddy.

Chapter Three

CLARE Davis worked in a department store within the Mall of America. As a visual design manager, she was responsible for making the entire three-level store look beautiful. She dressed mannequins, assembled vendor displays, and got the new stock out on the floor in a timely manner.

Clare trekked the women's section with an armload of designer sportswear. After last night's bizarre happenings and her subsequent wine binge, Clare was nursing the mother of all hangovers and shocked she was upright and breathing.

Hot on her heels was her assistant Stephen Nolan carrying his own stack of clothing. At age forty, Stephen was a whirl of frenetic energy fueled by nachos and cheese puffs. An impeccable dresser, he had the type of long limbs and slender body that looked good in everything. A receding hairline was his lone physical shortcoming. Clare listened to his daily obsessions about whether to shave his head au naturel, or throw caution to the wind and let nature take its course. Other than that tiny flaw, Clare adored Stephen and considered him her best friend.

As they walked the aisle, Stephen steadily yammered on about how cool it was that her online petition against one of their clothing vendors had gone viral. Last time Clare checked her email, there were more than one hundred thousand signatures urging a boycott of Renwalt Industries. The large wholesaler used overseas child labor and dangerous chemicals to manufacture their clothing.

"You're helping change the world, hon," Stephen said. There was pride in his voice. "You're my hero, Clare Davis."

Clare didn't feel like a hero. The information she'd shared with a few colleagues had turned into a massive crusade. She was in the running for a promotion. A rare buyer's position had opened in women's fashion, and she was perfect for the job. The interviewing process had gone well. She had the proper credentials and strong recommendations from her regional director and one of the buyers on the team. However, a smear campaign against a vendor, no matter how true, would not look good for her.

Midway through the aisle, Clare stopped short to glare at a mannequin dressed in a two-piece swimsuit. Bald and clutching a condom, the mannequin's missing wig was stuffed into her swim bottoms.

Caught off-guard, Stephen rammed into Clare's back. "Whoops. Didn't mean to run you over. What gives?"

Nodding at the dark fringe of hair peering out the suit leg holes, fresh pain shot into her pounding brain.

"Yikes," Stephen said. "Bikini wax to women's swim-wear. Stat!"

Clare laughed. This was what she loved about Stephen. No matter how bad the day, he always made her feel better.

Cocking his head to the side, he studied the scene as if he were looking at fine art. "I have to give creative points. Last week's group groping in lingerie showed more skill, but this has a certain ballsy flair."

"Edgy, yet tasteless," Clare agreed.

"Don't you know it. The piece practically screams, 'My mommy doesn't love me and now you asshats get to clean up my crap.'"

With a dramatic sigh, Stephen dumped his armload of clothes on a nearby table. Clare did the same. He turned to her with a pained expression. "Speaking of crap, I hate to be the bearer of bad news, but Jason Robey got your promotion."

Every muscle in Clare's body tensed. As far as she knew, Jason Robey hadn't applied for the position. "I didn't think he was interested," she said.

"He wasn't. They begged him to take it and coughed up a signing bonus. Act surprised when they tell you, though. I swore to that new girl in HR I wouldn't breathe a word to anyone. I don't want her to think she can't trust me."

Clare's mouth filled with the bitter taste of acid. "It's that petition. I knew it would kill my chances."

Stephen wagged his finger. "Not true. Word is the job was yours until Joanna put her two cents in."

Joanna Schram was the department store manager. A large, middle-aged woman, she had an abundance of arm flab and a shortage of compassion for those under her tight-fisted command.

Stephen laid a sympathetic hand on Clare's shoulder. "I'm sorry, hon. You've been severely Schramed."

A sharp pain worked its way deep between Clare's shoulder blades. She knew Joanna didn't like her, she was forever knit-picking and micromanaging everything Clare did, but she never thought she'd pull something like this. "Joanna is such a backstabbing witch," she said to Stephen.

"What did I ever do to her?"

The words barely left Clare's mouth when from behind, she heard the store manager's nasally throat clearing. Stephen's brows rose. "Holy mutha," he mouthed.

They both turned to face her, Stephen taking a step back.

With hands on round hips, Joanna's mouth was set in a hard line as she cast a withering glare at the mannequin, and then at Clare. "Apparently, you have too much time on your hands."

Clare felt her jaw drop. "Joanna, you can't believe I had anything to do with this."

"I find you idly gossiping. What else can I think?"

The pain between Clare's shoulders burned. "We're going to fix it."

"See that you do. Consider this a verbal warning." Before lumbering off, Joanna cut her eyes to Stephen, drilling in her point.

Stephen involuntarily shuddered. "Dreadful woman. Gives me the creeps. How long do you suppose she was standing behind us?"

Long enough, Clare feared as she dug the wig out of the mannequin's suit and gave it to Stephen. He had a thoughtful look as he arranged the wig. "Joanna has to be the reincarnation of Dracula. Who else terrorizes people and sucks the will to live from them?"

Dracula sounded about right to Clare. Joanna was the type of person who made you want to bury a stake in your own heart. Lord knew you couldn't please her. For the past three years she'd done her best trying. It was humiliating to work for someone whose sole mission was to find fault with everything she did.

She yanked a beach cover-up from the rack, tearing off a button. The hanger hit the floor with a clang. "I hate this job," she said.

Stephen gave her a thin smile. "Me too, but it pays for our wine."

A tiny moan escaped her. Gawd, she needed her wine. A glass or two every night helped take the edge off her miserable life. Last night she was so freaked over the accident that she drank two bottles. One glass after another disappeared until she more or less passed out. Around dawn she woke with a hammering head. A handful of aspirin got her on her feet. She couldn't make her apartment rent without a full paycheck.

So here she was, tugging and fixing a display with Stephen, adding a floppy hat and a straw tote to go with the cover-up. She stood back scrutinizing their work. Something was missing. There needed to be more color. Spying a turquoise necklace on a table next to Stephen, she asked him to hand it to her.

He didn't move. His attention was across the room, most likely on someone's outfit he had an issue with. Nudging him out of his daze, she pointed at the table. "Stephen, the necklace?"

He turned to her, giddy with excitement. "How do I look? Duh. Fabulous, of course. But how about my teeth? Any gunk?"

He bared a mouthful of teeth at her.

"Nothing but pearly whites," she confirmed.

"I'm so nervous. This is the *one*, I can feel it." He checked his breath. "Good, Lord. Quick, I need a mint."

Stephen fell in love at least weekly. Since it was Friday, he was due. Handing over her breath mints, Clare scanned the area. "I don't see him."

"Over my shoulder. Nordic God. Eleven o'clock."

Standing on tiptoes, she craned for a look at this god who had Stephen's panties in a bunch. The only people she saw was a woman in support hose pawing through the sales table and a teenager texting on his phone.

Stephen was nearly vibrating out of his skin. "Stuck-up Megan was drooling over him, trying to get his attention, when I caught him staring at me. We sooo had a moment."

Megan Gorman worked in the shoe department. Clare looked across the aisle in that direction and the ground fell out from under her. Making a beeline her direction was the man she'd hit with her car last night. She ducked behind Stephen, disbelief and horror in her groan.

"Sweetie? What's wrong?" he asked. "You look absolutely pasty."

"That's *him*."

Wheeling around, Stephen gave the man a critical once-over. "That's Mr. Tall, handsome, and technically dead?"

Clare cringed. "What do you suppose he wants?"

Stephen pulled a few wisps of hair forward. "A date, I hope."

d

As Ransom approached, he saw the color drain from Clare's stunned face. He flashed a smile. "Clare! What are the odds?"

"How do you know my name?"

"I heard the paramedic talking to you."

"But you were…" Her voice trailed off.

"Dead?" Ransom tapped his ear. "Hearing's the last to go."

Clare's assistant squeezed between them and offered Ransom his hand. "Hi. Stephen Nolan. And you are?"

"Ransom Mayes." He put some warmth into the handshake. "I'm the guy Clare ran over with her car."

Clare coughed hard into her hand. Her assistant seemed to take the news in stride. Smiling sweetly, he asked, "There aren't any permanent scars or bodily malfunctions, I hope?"

Ransom liked Stephen. Forthright guy. But he was here for Clare and growing impatient. All this chitchat was taking too long. The sooner he got her away from the store, the better.

Clare was regaining her color. "I'm sorry about last night," she said to him. "Are you sure you're okay?"

"I'm excellent." To prove it, he did a slow spin in front of her, arms out. "See, everything's where it's supposed to be."

"And then some," Stephen cooed.

Clare stared at Ransom. He noted her dilated pupils and heightened breathing. It was his eyes. They were mesmerizing, or so he'd often been told. Startling bright green, few had the will to turn away. Thankfully, Clare too seemed susceptible. This would make things much easier for both of them.

He purposely held her stare. "I need a favor. A ride."

Blinking once, she put a hand on her hip, looking

skeptical. "A ride where?"

"Not far."

Her eyes narrowed. "Where?"

"Hayward."

"Wisconsin?" Stephen asked. Ransom confirmed, and Stephen let go with a low whistle. He looked at Clare. "My cousin has a cabin near Hayward. It's way up north in Muskie country, where everyone talks about the big one." He winked at Ransom and Clare rolled her eyes. "Are you a fisherman, Mr. Mayes?"

"Not especially," he acknowledged. The truth was he had friends in Hayward, one in particular he wanted Clare to meet. Besides, Hayward was the perfect refuge. Small enough to keep track of anyone new to town, yet with a population of over two thousand, it had food, gas, and a couple motels. Everything they needed while he figured out how best to proceed.

"Get your coat," Ransom told Clare. "The sooner we're on the road, the better."

Clare didn't get her coat. She folded her arms and gaped at him as if he'd suggested she light her hair on fire. "Let me get this straight. You need a ride to Hayward? Hayward, Wisconsin? And you want me to take you there?"

"We can save time if you give me your car keys. I'll meet you at the door."

A long moment passed between, and then she gave a short bark of laughter. "Good one," she said, and went back to her work.

Ransom watched her fiddle with the bloody mannequin. Why wasn't she getting her things? Hadn't he made it obvious they needed to leave? The way she ignored him made him think she had no intention of doing what he'd asked.

He took a better look at his charge. Long, loose brown curls. Pretty face, delicate complexion. A stubborn chin he had to smile at. And for the first time in longer than he could remember, Ransom felt something like pride. Oh, he'd have fun making her regret this refusal, but all the same he was proud of her.

Stephen gazed moony-eyed at him. "I'll drive you wherever you want to go."

Clare leveled her assistant with a stern look. "We have work to do. Mr. Mayes can take the bus."

Ransom was getting nowhere and feared he might be running out of time. The men would come for her, of that he was clear. Stepping in front of her, he watched those big blue eyes coolly assess him. "I didn't want to point out the obvious, but you owe me," he said.

The air around them intensified. She blew out a breath as if collecting her thoughts. "I couldn't be happier you're not hurt, but I'm not taking you anywhere."

"What? Why not?" His tone was sharper than he intended. This was not the answer he expected.

Irritation showed on Clare by the way she snapped out a beach towel. "This is ridiculous. I don't know you."

"What's to know? I'm a nice guy. Here, you want to see some identification?" Ransom pulled out his wallet, handing her his student identification card.

Clare meticulously examined the card with Stephen breathing over her shoulder. She looked at him. "University of Minnesota. What are you studying?"

"Human beings."

An odd look crossed her face. Had he said something inappropriate? He'd been told he could be too literal.

Clare handed back his I.D. "I mean, what's your major?"

Oh. Got it. She was asking about his career plans. "I sit in on a few classes that interest me. Art and history mostly."

She snorted as if he was a complete joke, and he grinned at her. "Clare Davis, are you judging me?"

Her face turned bright red, and she swallowed hard. He could see the wheels turning inside her head. "N-no."

"Don't lie. You think I'm rich and have it easy."

Her chin lifted. "You can do whatever you want. I have to work, and hopefully you won't judge me for that."

Stephen grimaced and gave him a sympathetic look. She was a prickly little thing, lots of backbone. Too bad he wasn't in the mood for backbone. What he was in the mood for was saving her keister. It'd be a big help if she'd cooperate. Either way, he wasn't leaving without her.

Moving to a nearby table, Clare sorted through a tangled heap of jeans. Ransom followed her to the table and Stephen followed Ransom. "If you weren't working, would you give me a ride to Hayward?" he asked.

She heaved an enormous sigh but said nothing. He was wearing her down, he could feel it. It wouldn't take much to sway her.

Stephen folded clothes alongside Clare. Ransom noticed an easy rapport between them. The way Stephen teased made her laugh and relax. Hmm. Maybe the assistant was the key to getting Clare to do what he wanted.

The next time Stephen looked at Ransom, which was often, Ransom focused his energy on him. The man nearly passed out from joy. "Tell me, Stephen, is a simple ride too much to ask?"

"I don't see how," Stephen said, despite Clare's objecting scowl. "You did run him over, hon," he told her. "A ride with a gorgeous man to set the score straight seems like a no-brainer to me."

Her scowl deepened and she clapped her hands over her ears. "All right! I'll give him a ride when our shift is over."

"Not an option," Ransom said. "We need to leave now."

Clare openly stared at him. "What's with you? Do I have to talk slower? I'm *working*. I can't leave."

Nostril's flaring, she was about to say something more when Stephen gave her a nudge. He nodded past Ransom, his tone serious. "Time to gather the children."

Clare's eyes anxiously darted about as if she were looking for a place to hide. He could tell whatever was heading their way wasn't good.

Turning, Ransom saw a dour-faced woman in a boxy gray suit marching toward them, clipboard in hand. Suddenly, his day looked brighter. He faced Clare with a smile. "Let me guess. The boss?"

"You need to go," Clare told him.

Folding clothes with renewed vigor, Stephen agreed. "Save yourself from the blood-sucking demon. She acts like it's everyone's fault her husband divorced her for someone human."

At Stephen's words, tears sprang into Clare's eyes. Stephen looked perfectly horrified. "Oh, hon, I'm sorry. I didn't think." With a pained expression, he turned to Ransom. "A despicable man shattered poor Clare's heart. A real player. *Married*. Awful beast."

Clare's eyes went wide. "Stephen!"

Blinking, he thought back a moment before wincing. "Disregard that last bit," he told Ransom. "The mouth floweth before the brain thinketh."

The clack of heels on linoleum got louder behind him, and Ransom could see in Clare's eyes how much she wanted him to leave. He folded his arms. Not happening. Life was finally handing him a break.

The woman approached the group and stood next to him, her expression bleak as she eyed Clare. "Is there a problem?"

Clare straightened. "It's resolved. Mr. Mayes is leaving."

"Not resolved," Ransom said to the woman. Reading the badge pinned to her lapel, he smiled broadly. "Joanna. A beautiful name. I called my dog Joanna."

Stephen sputtered, choking back laughter, and Clare looked like she was thinking of ways to cause him pain. Not amused, the store manager peered over her glasses at him. "How may I be of service, Mr. Mayes?"

"That's big of you, Joanna." He gave her his this-means-a-lot-to-me nod. "The short story is Clare ran me over last night with her car. She was distracted and didn't look behind her."

Joanna's gaze shifted from Ransom to a flabbergasted Clare. "If this is true—"

"It's true," said Ransom cutting her off. "But I'm fine.

No harm done. My concern is for Clare and her state of mind. I know what distracted her."

Clare blanched a sickly gray as every head swiveled her way.

"You see, Joanna," Ransom continued. "Clare recently learned she was sleeping with a married man. A *player*. It must be devastating to have someone you deeply care about lie to your face every day, betraying your love and your trust." He paused, slowly shaking his head, staring directly at Joanna. "Can you imagine the heartache?" he asked her.

The room around them grew still as Joanna's ruddy complexion deepened to dark purple. The knuckles on her hands turned white holding the clipboard, and she appeared on the verge of implosion.

"Holy freaking shit," Stephen said, and clamped a hand over his mouth.

Clare looked beyond speech or rational thought. Grabbing a metal sales sign, she flung it at Ransom with all her might. The sign deflected off his shoulder and hit Joanna, tearing a one-inch gash across her forehead.

Chapter Four

EXITING the mall, Ransom zipped his parka against the harsh wind and shoved his hands inside his pockets. With a sharp eye out for trouble, he trailed Clare as she crossed the parking lot with coattails flapping, heels digging into the packed snow. It was pretty much a guarantee the cardboard box she carried contained her personal belongings from work.

Trotting alongside her, he greeted her with a friendly 'hey there.' Startled, her eyes went wide and then narrowed with recognition. "You!"

"I know you're upset, but I need a ride."

"You got me fired! I'm not taking you anywhere."

Weaving between the rows of parked cars, she marched along ignoring him. Ransom followed, matching her increased clip.

"Good. We need to pick up the pace," he told her.

"Get away from me," she said from over her shoulder. She pushed the remote, unlocking her Camry.

Ransom opened the back door and the corners of her mouth tipped downward. "I'm not helping you. Find someone else."

"I can't. Everyone's working."

That earned him a dirty look. She pitched the box onto the backseat, rattling the contents. Slamming the door shut, she wrenched the driver's side open about to get in when Ransom caught her arm. "Can I explain?"

Yanking from his grip, she glared at him, the wind whipping her hair in a maddened frenzy. "Okay. Explain why you got me fired."

He held up his hands. "Whoa. Your temper got you fired, not me. I would've gotten you a day off with pay."

She shook her head. "You're insane."

"I might be the only person you know who isn't."

"Ha! And you're delusional."

Ransom fought a smile. She looked like a spitting kitten, fur rising as she stood her ground. He resisted a strong urge to comfort her with a hug. Not a good idea, he reminded himself. Riled women knew a lot about where to cause men the most pain. No need to repeat that lesson.

He asked, "What would've happened if you hadn't thrown a sign at your boss?"

Fury darkened her eyes. "I threw the sign at *you*. I didn't mean to hit her."

"Fair enough. I'll rephrase the question. What would've happened if you hadn't thrown anything, and let the experience play out? "

"You were making her mad."

"Making her mad, or making you mad?"

She shifted on her feet. "You had no right to say those things. They were private, and none of your business."

"What I said was hurtful?"

"You know darn well it was."

"You felt betrayed by your lover and by me. Right?"

She pushed back her hair, exasperated. "Why are you messing with me? What do you want?"

"I want you to consider how your boss feels. Her

husband abandoned their marriage. Don't you suppose she feels the same betrayal? You two have a lot in common."

Clare snorted. "She hates me."

"No. Her heart's been broken, same as yours. That type of deep emotion fogs the mind. When you're together you're like mirrors, each reflecting pain, expanding it until it's this huge wedge between you. By staying calm and not adding to the pain, you would've made it easier for your boss to process her feelings."

Clare rolled her eyes. "Thank you, Dr. Know-Nothing. Better stick to art classes, you couldn't be more wrong. Joanna's a mean, hateful person. She's been looking for a way to fire me forever."

"And you provided her with one. But what do you care? You hate your job."

"How did you know that?"

He grinned. "Took a stab. Everyone hates their jobs."

"You're arrogant, Mr. Mayes."

"Doesn't make me wrong."

She tilted her head, eyeing him. "How old are you?"

"Old."

Amusement hinted at her lips. Ransom knew he didn't look more than twenty. "Why don't you drive yourself to Hayward?" she asked.

"Can't. My license was suspended."

"Let me guess. Underage drinking."

"Nope. Hit a guy with my car." He met her astonished stare. "Ironic, huh? Broke his leg, but I didn't kill him."

What Ransom wasn't about to tell her was he had

run over the man on purpose—a doctor. He remembered the event as if it had happened yesterday. He'd jumped the curb with his car and aimed for him. The doctor bounced off the left front fender and rolled onto the grassy median. A moment later the abortion clinic across the street exploded, sending tongues of fire skyward. Had he not intervened, the doctor would have died. The presiding judge on the case didn't see it the same way, and suspended Ransom's license. Neither did the judge see the last minute change of heart of the man who had set the explosives, but he did.

A long sigh escaped her. "I know I'll regret this, but get in."

She didn't have to tell him twice. He slid into the passenger seat and strapped on the seatbelt. Clare turned the ignition and backed out of the parking space. "What's in Hayward that's so important, anyway?" she asked him.

"A medicine man."

"Of course, there is," she grumbled, more or less to herself. "Guess I should be grateful we're not after Big Foot."

"Big Foot isn't in Hayward," he said, and her eyes cut to him. He smiled. "It's a joke, Clare. I don't know where Big Foot lives."

"Funny," she said dryly, turning into traffic. Her chin lifted. "Joanna wouldn't have given me the day off."

Ransom shrugged. "We'll never know, will we?"

d

Twenty minutes later, Ransom stood inside the small foyer of Clare's apartment building. He was holding the box with her belongings. Pausing to collect her mail,

Clare shuffled through the envelopes achingly slow as if paid to waste time. He would've preferred driving straight to Hayward, but she stubbornly refused until she changed out of her skirt and heels.

Clare trudged up the stairs to the second floor, and he followed, her skirt making swishing sounds with each step. The stairs emptied into a dimly lit hallway with three sets of doors on either side. Keys in hand, she unlocked the first door and hesitated, giving him a sheepish look. "Wait here. I wasn't expecting company and won't be longer than five minutes, tops."

Grabbing the box from his hands, she hip-checked the door and disappeared inside. Ransom stared at the closed door and felt a grin twitch his lips. It was laughable, her thinking he'd care if her apartment was a mess. She had no clue how many times he'd already been inside her place.

He took hold of the knob and stepped into the familiar living room, with its makeshift sewing station along the far wall. To his left was a tiny U-shaped kitchen. An open snack bar with two stools separated the space. Usually tidy, today the sink was stacked with dirty dishes. Melted ice cream pooled on the counter around the open container.

Clare was in the living room when he walked in, clutching two empty wine bottles. She tensed at the sight of him. "What are you doing in here? I told you to wait in the hallway."

"I don't want to wait out there," he said. "I don't want to wait at all." Ransom looked at the coffee table covered with crumpled chip bags and a half-eaten pizza. "Can't you pick up this stuff later?"

Clare's left eye twitched and she pressed on the offending nerve. "You're giving me a migraine."

He held up a hand, fingers spread. "Five minutes. That's what you said. You've used two."

"Fine," she snapped, dropping the bottles. Muttering under her breath, she stalked to the bedroom. The door shut with a bang.

Feisty. A good sign, he thought, especially given her dispirited history. Heading into the kitchen, he looked in the refrigerator and frowned at the contents: a six-pack of soda, energy drinks, three more bottles of wine, a shriveled cucumber, and a package of moldy taco shells. A quick scan of the above freezer told him she ate a lot of pizza and ice cream.

Turning toward the window, he noticed a potted plant on the sill. The leaves were withered and brown and the soil bone dry. He gave the plant a shot of water before moving to her sewing station.

This area was a permanent disaster, but it was here he knew she was happiest. Paper patterns and silky fabrics were piled high on the ironing board, and threads and bits of material littered the carpet. The pencil sketches tacked to the wall featured elegant negligees and fancy women's undergarments. The renderings were good, artistic and original, with scraps of lace and fabric pinned to each.

Leaning in for a closer look, his foot bumped against a laser printer beneath the cutting table. Bending to straighten the printer, he noticed a sheet of parchment in the tray. It was a poem of some kind:

My dearest Ashley,
Mother of my children, keeper of my heart. Each

year we're together finds me more in love. Happy anniversary, darling.

Jason.

Ransom saw similar poems with different names tied to elaborately gift-wrapped packages. They were carefully staggered on a bookshelf to keep from crushing the handtied bows. The top shelf contained books, the greatest share were of fashion and design from the Victorian era. The solo exception was a photo album.

Curious, Ransom selected the album and paged through it. Professionally taken, the images were of Clare and a good-looking man in a grassy field, cuddling, holding hands, gazing into each other's eyes. She wore a diamond on her left ring finger, and looked happy and healthy, full of life. These were pictures of the old Clare, the woman she was before the darkness hollowed her heart and filled her with a sorrow she could not escape on her own. That's why he was here. That's why *they* were here, too.

Putting the album back, he peered through the living room blinds. Her apartment was to the rear of the building with a view of the parking lot. Not noticing anything suspicious, he breathed slightly easier. Of course, the men in the black SUV could be watching her from the gas station across the street. Or the bus stop on the corner. They could be circling her block this minute.

He pulled the blinds tight. What was taking her so long? He stared at her bedroom door, and willed her to appear. Five minutes was ten minutes ago. Ransom put his ear to the door, and wrapped twice. "Tick-tock, Clare. Let's go."

She responded with a low moan. Ransom peered in. Fully dressed in blue jeans and a bulky sweater, Clare was curled in a fetal position on top of the bed. Her face was drawn and pinched. Dark circles rimmed her eyes. She gave him a guilty look. "Can't we go tomorrow? I don't feel like a three-hour drive."

"A deal's a deal," he said.

He opened the shades and bright sun streamed through the window. Wincing, Clare put a hand up blocking the light. "Hey, who asked you to do that?"

The room smelled foul. "Did you puke?" he asked.

She closed her eyes and swallowed, perspiration beading her upper lip. With a wave of her hand she said, "Clothes basket in the corner."

Ransom did a hesitant inspection of the basket. Yep. She did a first-rate job. Get some fresh air and food into her, and she'd be good as new.

He slid back the window as far as it would go. Freezing cold air rushed in. Grabbing the basket, he pushed the smelly mess out the window, dropping it onto the sidewalk below. The basket bounced, dumping the contents, before rolling against the building.

Clare was up on her elbows, glaring at him. "Those were my clothes."

"Oh, I'm sorry. Were you going to wear them again?"

Her lips pressed together. "I suppose not. But could you stop? I feel horrible. I've had the morning from hell and I need a minute. Okay?"

"You've had eighteen," he said with some edge in his tone.

Crossing to her closet, he flung open the doors. Raking through her wardrobe, he selected a hooded peacoat and wool scarf. He tossed them on the bed before grabbing a pair of leather boots with flat heels.

Alarmed, Clare got to her feet. "What are you doing? Get out of my stuff. What kind of weirdo are you?"

Roughly pushing the boots into her hands, Ransom stared at her. "I wouldn't ask you to do something if it weren't important. You said you'd drive me."

She fell silent, her blues eyes judging his sincerity. Man, how he wished he could tell her everything. He had a lot of leeway in his job, but this was not his call to make. He had come to trust the process and hoped someday she would too. One step at a time, he reminded himself.

Folding her arms, there was finality in her tone when she spoke to him. "So there's no misunderstanding, once I take you to the medicine man, we're even. I don't owe you any more favors."

"Agreed," he said.

Chapter Five

TRAFFIC flowing north was light, and the roads were dry with occasional icy patches. Ransom slumped in the seat of Clare's Camry with his eyes closed listening to the sounds of the engine. People missed that, the everyday sounds, mundane, yet necessary to make life go. They mostly had no idea about what they were thinking, or seeing, or doing.

He could feel Clare's eyes on him. "Awfully quiet," she said. "Are you okay?"

Nodding, he turned toward the window. Judging from Clare's anxious stare, he knew she had sensed his dismal mood. Emotions unchecked were contagions, easily infecting anyone within his surroundings. The evidence spoke for itself. When he was too high, those who were stable found themselves laughing uncontrollably. For the unstable, the feeling of euphoria caused reckless abandon. Unaccustomed to this natural state, they often believed they could fly. A few had jumped from non-survivable heights.

If his emotions were low, people drugged themselves numb or took their own lives. Too high or too low, the results were the same, leaving him to conclude people around him were safer if he kept his emotions in check.

Opening the window, Ransom breathed in the crisp air, clearing his mood. Clare's demeanor brightened. "I feel like singing," she told him. "Mind if I turn on the radio?"

Ransom smiled. "I'd like that."

Clare found an oldies station, and for the next thirty minutes hummed along, singing a verse or two of the songs she knew. He liked her voice. It was earthy and strong.

"I don't know what's gotten into me," she said. "I don't sing. My voice isn't the best."

"You sound great. You should sing more often."

A small smile tugged her lips, and he could feel her relaxing toward him. Too bad he had to rile her again. They were finally getting along. But what kind of guardian would he be if he didn't do his job?

He cleared his throat. "Why were you at the club last night?"

She stiffened, as he knew she would, her grip tightening on the steering wheel. "Why do you want to know?"

He gave her a noncommittal shrug. "Just killing time, and thought we could talk about the experience that brought us together."

Her brows shot up. "Experience? Is that what you call what happened?"

"What would you call it?"

"A miracle!"

Ransom grunted. "That's a tad dramatic."

"You weren't breathing. The paramedic couldn't find a pulse. Everyone thought you were dead! I was so scared." She looked over at him flushing with embarrassment. "I hate to say it, but I was mainly scared for myself. I'm sorry."

"Don't apologize for honesty. Why were you scared?"

"*Why?* What if you would've died?"

"What if I would've?"

Worry creased her brow as she thought about the question. "I guess I was wondering if your family would sue me. Do you have a family?"

Ransom considered a moment. How long had it been since anyone asked him about his family? At least a millennia, or longer. He shook away the thought. Clare was his family now, and he'd give his life for her without question. "No one related to me would ask you for money," he said. "What else were you afraid of?"

"If you died?"

He nodded.

She blew out a breath. "I don't know. It was horrible. Everything happened so fast. I hadn't been drinking, but who knows? I might've been charged with manslaughter and gone to prison. My whole life would've changed."

"How was your life before you ran me over?"

"What do you mean?"

"Were you happy?"

She eyed him. "Not especially."

"How do you feel now?"

Her eyes widened. "Grateful." She looked at him. "I feel grateful."

"So running into me wasn't such a horrible thing. You should thank me. Show *me* some of that gratitude."

Her brow arched, but he could tell she was biting back a grin, enjoying his teasing. "You have to be so smug all the time?"

"It's my special talent."

"Well, you're incredibly gifted."

She gave him a real smile, and damn she looked

radiant. How he would love to keep her in this heightened energy, but that would be a mistake. There were no shortcuts, as he'd painfully learned. She'd soar on her own when she was ready.

As if sensing something had changed between them, Clare straightened, shifting her gaze to the road ahead. She was quiet for a moment, her eyes reddening on the verge of tears. "You asked why I was at the club. The truth is I followed a man there, my lover. Or I thought he was until I realized he was using me."

Ransom's heart ached. There was so much pain inside her. "Why did you follow him?" he asked.

Clare gave a slight shrug. "He told me he was going home to work, but I wondered if he was lying."

"And you found him at the club?"

She nodded, miserable. "With another woman."

He turned in his seat toward her. "Is this the first time you suspected him?"

Her brows furrowed. "I suppose there were things that should've registered... Hindsight, right?"

She looked so sad he hated to press her, but she was so close to unlocking her true identity. "Why did you follow him?" he asked. "What made last night different?"

"I followed him because I had this sinking feeling in the pit of my stomach." She swallowed hard, as if reliving the bitterness of the moment. "I was extremely hurt when I caught him with her, but now that I think about it, I would've been surprised if I hadn't."

Ah, finally they were getting somewhere. Ransom asked, "What told you something was off?"

She shook her head slightly. "Intuition, I guess."

"And where does intuition come from?"

"Inside me? Kind of like an idea that won't go away."

Ransom flashed his brightest smile. She'd earned it. "Intuition is the giant bullshit meter that hangs above your soul's door. Everything entering this space has to pass through the meter for inspection. It's a hug and hello from your inner guide."

She frowned. "You're talking about God."

"I'm talking about the guide inside that won't steer you wrong. Call it what you want: Source, a hunch, a feeling, call it Benjamin Franklin if you want to. The title doesn't matter. What matters is you pay attention, because the first step to a peaceful, joy-filled life is to listen to your intuition."

"Why didn't I hear my intuition right away? Why did everything have to get so bad?"

"Simple. Intuition isn't into drama. It doesn't yell, or scream, or boss you around. You have to be quiet to hear the message, because it's quiet and sounds a lot like common sense. Do you know what common sense is?"

She blew out an impatient sigh. "Everyone knows that."

"Does everyone know it's an inner sense common with the Creator to know without doubt your path and when you're on it?"

Clare's long lashes fluttered. "I've never heard it put that way."

That was the problem. Everyone on the planet had common sense, but few valued what was always accurate and free. They were chasing the mythical rare.

He looked out the window. The towns they passed

were getting smaller and the woods between them denser. Another hour and he'd be with his old friend again. Sinking into the seat getting comfortable, he closed his eyes. "Let me know when we get to Hayward."

He didn't dare divulge the difficulties awaiting her once they arrived.

Chapter Six

TWO miles north of Hayward, Ransom instructed Clare to turn by a peeling, hand-painted sign advertising a healing center. The rutted, snow-packed driveway cut through thick woods. It took all her strength to hang onto the steering wheel and keep the Camry on the road.

The driveway bent sharply into a clearing revealing a ranch-style house sided with weathered plywood. The porch was stacked with a neat pile of wood, and smoke billowed from a metal chimney pipe. A white pole shed was next to the house. Screwed to the door, another hand-painted sign announced the healing center. Around the corner, an ATV with a snow blade was up on cement blocks. The fenders and rear tire were missing. Explained the rough driveway, Clare thought.

She pulled in front of the shed and parked next to a silver Lexus. The luxury sedan seemed out of place with the rest of the setting. "Who is this guy, anyway?" she asked Ransom. "You called him a medicine man?"

"Eugene White helps people with their problems."

"What kind of problems?"

"Depends," he said, pulling on his coat. "Sometimes he just likes to piss people off."

"And he gets paid?" Clare was floored.

Laughing, Ransom got out of the car, and leaned back in. "You coming? It'll be warmer inside than waiting for me out here."

"Why? How long will you be?"

"As long as it takes."

He flashed her that grin, the one he used before he was about to do something she didn't like. But in spite of her wariness, Clare had never seen a medicine man and her curiosity got the better of her. She grabbed her purse off the seat. "Stop grinning," she told him. "It's irritating."

"Yes, ma'am," he saluted. His green eyes sparkled with mischief as he held the door for her. "After you."

Clare stepped into a large, brightly lit room with white walls and a blue cement floor. The pungent odor of burning incense triggered her allergies. Rubbing itchy eyes, she steered clear of herbs drying on a rack, and followed Ransom to a small lobby with mismatched furniture. Scanning the different options with their peculiar stains, she decided on a metal folding chair.

On a bench across from her sat two women. One was elderly and frail-looking. Her gnarled hands worked the beads of a rosary. The younger woman seated next to her wore designer clothing Clare recognized. She gently rubbed the elder's back as the woman gagged, trying to force down a small glass of dark liquid. "You're doing great, Mom. Almost finished. A few more sips."

The elder belched, and drained the glass with a shudder. Clare involuntarily shuddered with her. She was about to suggest to Ransom they leave and give the women privacy, when Ransom wedged himself onto the bench between them. The sick woman did as best she could to slide over, and the perturbed daughter scooted forward half off the seat. Clare could've crawled under hers. Ransom was the only one who looked comfortable.

He made their introductions, and with reservation, the daughter made theirs. She was Gretchen, and her mother was Ava.

Ransom smiled broadly at the women and announced, "Clare ran me over with her car last night."

The women's brows arched in unison and their heads swiveled Clare's way. She felt herself turn eight shades of red. Was he going to tell this story to everyone they met? She wished she would've stayed in the car.

Gretchen surveyed Ransom with a wary eye. "At least you didn't get hurt."

"Not true. I was dead," he assured. "The paramedic on the scene said so. Isn't that right, Clare?"

Both women gaped in alarm, Clare inwardly groaned. The glint in his eye told her he enjoyed putting her on the spot.

"Did someone do CPR?" Gretchen asked.

Clare shook her head no. "He just...woke up."

The room got quiet as each woman privately mulled over a reasonable explanation for such a phenomenon.

Ava peered at him, curious. "Did you have a near-death experience?"

"What's a near-death?" he asked.

With considerable effort, Ava pulled herself straighter in order to look Ransom in the eye. "A friend of mine had a heart attack on the operating table. She told me she floated out of her body and saw the doctors working on her. She went through a dark tunnel and came out into a bright, white light where she felt safe and loved and didn't have pain. A voice told her she had to go back to her life. The next thing she remembered was waking in the recovery room. The doctors said she'd been clinically dead for seven minutes." Ava's expression turned hopeful. "Did you see a white light?" she asked him.

Ransom held her gaze. "Are you asking about heaven?"

Ava braced herself with a firm grip on her rosary. "I guess I am."

Clare caught herself leaning closer, intrigued as to what Ransom might say. From everything she'd read on the subject, heaven was a figment of the dying brain's imagination.

He smiled at Ava. "My beautiful woman. I don't know what you've been told, but heaven is where you find the best popcorn. Mmm." He licked his lips as if he could taste it. "It's hot and fresh and loaded with melted butter. And it's yours the second you think of it. In heaven there's no such thing as delay. You think it, and it's yours. You want to go somewhere, you're there. You're also clear about your purpose and what you're creating, so there's no suffering."

Ava eyed him. "I've heard our family greets us when we die. Is that true?"

"Yes. Your family and friends are with you, the ones who have passed and the higher spirit of those on earth."

"What about our pets?" Gretchen asked.

"They are there, too. Heaven is where you rest and have fun with loved ones."

Clare could feel her eyes rolling. What a load of malarkey. Her grandmother used to believe the same way, and where had it gotten her? Riddled with cancer and screaming bloody murder on her deathbed.

Clearing her throat, Clare said, "I've read studies that prove a portion of the brain is triggered during death giving what is commonly called the near-death experience.

There's no scientific evidence of an afterlife. More likely than not, death is the end. Nothing else happens."

Ava's face fell, and she sagged back against the bench. Gretchen cast Clare a who-asked-you glare, and Clare lifted her chin. Could she help if they were this easily duped? And what was Ransom's game anyway? If she were dying, she'd appreciate the truth and not false hope.

Ransom treated her to a wide, happy grin, which made her nervous. He said, "Scientists have isolated an area of the brain that helps in the mortal life process of dying, but they are incorrect in assuming nothing happens after death. The disconnection of spirit from the body happens. It's sort of like turning off the ignition before getting out of the car. Since science has yet to prove Spirit exists, they can't prove an afterlife, which technically is not afterlife."

Gretchen blinked her surprise. "What is it?"

"It's all the same—Life."

The elderly woman pressed her pale lips together. Something important was on her mind. She asked Ransom, "What if you're not allowed into heaven? What if God judges you unworthy?"

Gretchen was horrified. "Mom. Stop. You're a good person."

Silencing her daughter with an impatient wave, Ava's focus was on Ransom. Gently, he reached for her hand, and she didn't pull away. Searching her eyes, he said, "God does not judge. In your heart you know this is true. What would be his purpose?"

A haunted look came over Ava, a bottomless cavern of pain. This dark space Clare understood, and put a hand over her heart to still the panic rising in her.

"What if you've done something unforgiveable?" Ava asked, her voice a dry whisper.

Ransom shook his head. "God is *crazy* about you, and there's nothing you could do to change his mind about that. He knows each of us intimately, because we are his thoughts. We can be disappointed and fearful and a whole lot of things, but these are our thoughts and feelings. Love is God's prime thought. There's nothing to forgive in his eyes, and you are always with God."

The women listened to Ransom in open-eyed wonder. Clare remained unconvinced. The night she slashed her wrist she was utterly alone. Her misery so intense she didn't feel the razor cut through her skin. God wasn't with her, because there was no such thing.

Ava's voice trembled with emotion. "I'm afraid to die," she said.

Ransom squeezed her hand. "I know you are, but look at me. Back from the dead and no worse for wear."

She gave him a tight smile. "What you say sounds wonderful, but what about the devil? Doesn't he want to win us over?"

His brows furrowed. "Win us over?"

"You know. Steal our souls?"

"Ah, that devil." Ransom winked. "I'll tell you about the devil. He hates people who think about nice things, such as friendship, and grandchildren, and pretty daughters like the one you have here."

He let loose with a megawatt smile for Gretchen, and her sour face lit with delight. What was it about him, Clare wondered? His pile of bull charmed everyone he met.

Ransom said, "The devil's fickle and likes to be entertained. People who enjoy sunrises and star-filled nights, tending to gardens, or fishing, or music, or life in general, bore him to death. My advice? Keep your mind on Life's beautiful creations, and the devil will avoid you like the plague."

Ava peered down her nose at him, not amused. "Don't toy with me, young man. Is that true?"

"Every word." He crossed his heart for good measure.

Appearing satisfied, Ava rose and stood on uncertain feet. She said to her daughter, "Take me home."

Ransom and Gretchen each hooked an arm around her and together they shuffled to the door held open by Clare. Ava paused a moment catching her breath, a gleam in her eyes Clare had not seen before.

"You're blessed," the elderly woman told her. "You travel with one of God's special angels."

Clare looked at Ransom, who crossed his eyes and made a goofy face. What a weirdo. She shut the door on him and returned to her seat.

Ransom was no angel, not by a long shot. And what was the deal with Ava calling her blessed? What did she know? There hadn't been a lot of blessings in her life. Not since the night her fiancé took back his ring. Every man she dated since was a pale reflection of what she had. Until Keith. With him she dared to hope again, be vulnerable, take a chance. And look how that ended. A true blessing would be not to have to endure this terrible sadness.

Life was exhausting. She felt a hundred years old. Everything ached—her joints, her skin, her bones. The wine she drank never dulled the pain for long. Only one thought spoke peace to her. With the help of her therapist she had fought this notion, but lately found herself listening to its soothing whispers. How nice, it said, how wonderfully blissful to go to sleep and not wake. That would be heaven.

From outside, a vehicle revved to life pulling Clare from her thoughts. The sound was a lot like her Camry. She dug in her coat pocket for the keys. They weren't there. With heart pounding, she raced for the door and flung it open in time to see Ransom drive away with her car.

Chapter Seven

CLARE jumped up and down in the freezing cold, waving her arms, shouting at the top of her lungs, as she watched her car disappear down the driveway. She couldn't believe it. Ransom took her car! "Angel, my ass," she spouted. "The guy belongs in jail."

Grabbing her cellphone from her purse, she punched in the emergency number and got a 'no service' message. Damn redneck backwoods middle of nowhere!

She was about to run to the healing center for help, when a Native American man stepped out of the house, followed by a creature that looked like a wolf. The man had long gray hair tied in a ponytail, and a face as wrinkled and brown as a dried apple. He wore blue jeans and an insulated vest over an untucked shirt, and couldn't have weighed more than 140 pounds soaking wet.

The animal's ears pricked when she walked toward them, and he let out a couple warning barks. Keeping her distance, Clare stayed on the bottom porch step and looked up at the man. "Are you Eugene White?"

He squinted at her, sizing her up, his blue eyes as ageless and startling as Ransom's. "Could be," he said.

She waved her useless phone at him. "I can't get reception and I need to call the police. A man stole my car."

He leisurely leaned against the wall and lit a cigarette. Blowing smoke from the side of his mouth, he said, "That right."

That right? Why would she lie? Her patience waned.

Ransom would be three states away by the time the police were called.

"Do you have a phone I can use?" she asked, stepping onto the porch. A low growl erupted in the animal's throat and she quickly retreated. "Is that a wolf?"

Eugene blew another plume of smoke toward the ceiling. "What kind of a medicine man would I be without a wolf?" he asked.

He scratched the giant head. The animal rolled onto its back, legs in the air, waiting for a belly rub. He looked about as harmless as a newborn kitten.

Clare knew she'd been had. "He's not a wolf, is he?"

There was laughter in Eugene's eyes. "Naw, just messing with you. Old Roger is pure pussycat."

The dog thumped his tail when he heard his name and gave the medicine man's hand an affectionate lick. Clare felt about two inches tall.

Taking a last hit from the cigarette, Eugene crushed it out with the toe of his boot, and walked past her to the healing center. The dog trailed barely giving her a sniff.

Clare stood with hands on hips. "What about my car? I need to call the police."

"If you think so," he said from over his shoulder.

She watched stupefied as he and the dog disappeared inside the building. Had everyone gone insane today? Stomping into the center, she found Eugene in one of the healing rooms perched on a stool with arms folded.

A long, irritated breath escaped her. "May I use your phone?"

"Sure," his voice bright as he handed it over.

Anxious to make her call, Clare pressed the on button. Nothing happened. The phone was dead. She looked at him.

"Batteries might need charging," he admitted.

She wanted to hurl the blasted thing against the wall and watch it disintegrate into a million pieces. And what was worse, Eugene was grinning at her as if her misery was high entertainment.

She narrowed her eyes. "Something funny?"

"Woman, you are wound tighter than a goddamn clock," he said.

Clare stiffened. What was this guy's problem? "I've been trying to tell you my car was stolen and I need a phone."

"What you need is serious aligning. You've got yourself completely fucked up."

She was appalled. "What kind of medicine man swears and smokes cigarettes?"

"You think the force that powers the universe gives a shit about that? The people who take offense are those who don't know the Creator."

"Creator? Ha!" Clare had heard enough. "Who would create such a hateful world? Nothing but wars and disasters, and people who take their love away the second they don't get what they want. And don't bother praying for answers, because trust me, no one answers." She straightened, looking down her nose at him. "But you're right. If something is behind this madness, not only doesn't it care about your foul mouth, from what I can see it doesn't care about anything."

Eugene barked out a laugh. "Holy Christ, you're quite a pistol. Feel better?"

In spite of some embarrassment, she did feel better. Surprisingly lighter, as if a huge burden had lifted.

"Good." He patted the table. "Let's get to work."

Alarmed, Clare took a step back. "Ransom's your patient, not me." She felt herself frowning as she thought of him. "I don't get it. Why would he insist I bring him here and then take off?"

"Hell of a mystery," Eugene admitted, sounding more amused than mystified.

He snapped his fingers and a whoosh of fur sailed past Clare onto the table. The dog circled twice and plopped down with a grunt. The medicine man stroked the dog's thick fur with a calloused hand. "Roger's a goddamn energy whore, aren't you fella?"

The dog looked at him with large, round eyes, and wagged his tail. To Clare, he said, "I'll do a short demo with Roger as my client. If you decide you don't want a session, no skin off my ass."

Clare stubbornly folded her arms. "I'm not getting on that table. But I suppose there's no harm in watching you work on your dog."

"That's the spirit." Eugene gave Roger another friendly pat and asked her, "Do you know anything about energy work or the chakra system?"

"The what system?"

"Chakra. The word comes from an ancient language, and means "wheel". These energy centers are arranged vertically along the body's spine, and look something like mini tornadoes."

Clare gave him a blank look. "Energy centers? You lost me."

That got him thinking, and he rubbed his chin. "Okay,

let's keep this simple. Everything in the universe is made of energy vibrating at different speeds. Agreed?"

Of course she agreed. Scientific research had proven this fact.

"The way we process energy is through the chakras," he said. "With a fully functioning chakra system, the body is balanced physically, emotionally, mentally, and spiritually."

"What happens if the chakras aren't working the way they should?" she asked.

"That's an energy block, which causes a lot of god-damn pain."

Clare suffered with migraines throughout her life. Could they be caused by energy blocks?

"There are seven major chakras," he told her. "Each has a specific job and color association." He touched the dog's tailbone area. "This is the location of the root chakra, and the corresponding color is red. The root is our foundation and deals with survival instincts, our sense of security, and feelings of being grounded."

Eugene moved up Roger's spine, touching a spot a couple inches above the tailbone. "The sacral chakra," he said. "On people, it's found about two inches below the naval. The sacral primarily governs sexuality and relationships, as well as creativity and abundance. It's associated with the color orange."

Stopping mid-back, he looked at Clare. "The solar plexus. The color is yellow. Anchored within this chakra is our sense of self-worth and personal power, giving us confidence and the ability to control our lives."

Eugene touched the dog between the shoulder blades. "The heart chakra found mid-chest. The color is green.

This is the place of compassion, inner peace, our notion of joy and capacity to love."

So far throughout the demonstration the dog had been a rockstar. Tolerant and endlessly patient. Clare doubted she'd be as good-natured.

The medicine man moved to Roger's neck, touching the hollow area at the base of the throat. "The throat chakra color is blue and its main functions are creative self-expression and communication of true feelings."

He put his finger on the forehead between the animal's eyes. "The brow chakra, also called the third eye, is indigo blue. This is the center for intuition, imagination, and wisdom. It helps us focus and see the big picture."

Feeling for the center of the dog's head, Eugene said, "The crown chakra color is purple and represents union with the Creator. It leads us to deeper understanding, great knowledge, and inner bliss. Isn't that right, Roger?" He scratched behind the giant animal's ears, and the dog's back leg quivered.

Clare's interest was piqued. "How do the chakras take in energy?"

"Through the aura. The body has layers of energy vibrating at increasing rates. Some people can see different colors in the aura, but almost everyone can feel it."

"In what way?"

"If a person stands too close to you, how do you feel?"

"Uncomfortable, like they're in my space."

"That's because they're standing inside your individual aura, the space uniquely you."

Clare had to admit the concept was intriguing. Many times she'd backed away from someone feeling as if they'd crossed a personal line. This made her think of more questions. "How does the energy travel through the body?"

"Through an electromagnetic current, but it's a hell of a lot easier to show you how the energy system works than to explain it."

Palms down, the medicine man's hands hovered a foot above the dog's spine at the root and sacral chakras. He looked at Clare. "Life Force energy travels through my body and out the palm of my hands, helping open, connect, and balance Roger's energy system through his chakras."

The dog yawned and closed his eyes, and let out a contented sigh.

"Looks like Roger likes whatever you're doing," Clare said.

"Damn right, he does. He's got a bunch of congested energy and I'm helping him get rid of it."

Clare shifted on her feet. "Congested energy?"

"The energy gets stuck if the system is out of balance, and I feel it in my hands like pin pricks. A healthy system feels smooth to me. My hands get warm and tingly, and I can feel the chakras spinning."

Pin pricks and spinning chakras? This seemed highly doubtful to Clare. How could anyone feel something invisible?

The medicine man sat back on his stool assessing her. "Looks like you don't believe me. Why don't you give it a try?"

What? Heal the dog? The guy was crazy. She shook her head. "I'm not a healer."

Eugene's eyes lit with laughter, and Clare had the

notion it was at her expense, but she let him guide her hand over the dog's heart chakra, mid-chest. Not sure what was supposed to happen, she was shocked when her hand tingled and she felt spinning pressure against her palm. "This is weird," she said.

"Try Roger's root chakra," he suggested.

Moving her hand to the base of the dog's spine, she waited a moment and frowned. "It's not spinning. I don't feel anything."

With a snap of Eugene's fingers, the dog flipped onto his back where a suture line was visible on his lower abdomen. "Roger had surgery last week. Got caught pants down with the neighbor's beagle, didn't you old boy."

The dog licked his chops, pleased with himself. Clare couldn't help smiling at the giant beast. She held her hands over the surgical site as Eugene instructed, and was puzzled by what she felt. "There's a cold breeze coming out of the wound. Could that be right?"

"It's an energy leak," Eugene explained. "Traumas to the body such as surgeries, accidents, even the birthing process can cause leaks. If the leak isn't sealed, vital energy seeps through the opening and the body feels drained."

Fascinated, Clare watched the medicine man as he appeared to gather invisible energy around the wound. Placing both hands over the site, he held the position for about a minute, and invited her to recheck the site.

To her amazement, the cold draft was gone and her palms felt warm and tingly. She stared at the medicine man. "How did you do that?"

"The Creator heals, not me. I'm like a cord running between the power company and a lamp. The switch gets turned on when the person, or dog in this case, agrees to the healing."

"How do you know your dog agreed?"

"Look at him. He's a limp noodle."

Eugene took a dog treat from his pocket, and Roger swallowed it whole. With a snap of Eugene's fingers, Roger leapt off the table, shook his husky body, and disappeared from the room. The medicine man arched a questioning brow at her. "You ready?"

Clare looked at the vacated table, and she looked at Eugene. She looked out the window. An anxious sensation gnawed at her. Eugene seemed to read her mind. "Don't worry. Ransom will be back for you."

"How can you be sure?"

His eyes twinkled. "Call it a strong intuitive hunch."

Intuition, there was that word again. *The guide within,* Ransom had said. Turning inward, Clare put the question of Ransom's returning to her own intuition. Surprisingly, her gut instinct agreed with Eugene and she silently groaned.

Stretching onto the massage table, Clare's stomach was in knots. To his credit, Eugene didn't gloat. Grabbing a small bundle of dried plants, he held them out for her to see. Tied with string, they had a faint, sweet smell.

"This is a smudge stick made from herbs," he told her.

He placed the bundle on an abalone shell, and lit the end. A curl of smoke wafted upward. Using a long feather, he waved the smoke in every direction and over her heart while reciting prayers of gratitude.

The swirling aroma was pleasant enough, except her allergies kicked in. She wiped at watery eyes. "What's the purpose for this?"

"The feather combs the aura of blockages, and the smoke cleanses. We are welcoming Great Spirits, angels, and ancestors to our sacred space. We ask for their help with the healing."

Eugene continued with the smoke bath, brushing and cleansing, invoking special blessings on her behalf. Finally, he stubbed out the smudge stick and set it aside.

As the medicine man passed his hands over Clare's body, she felt a rippling motion from the top of her head to her feet. The sensation was surprising, but not uncomfortable.

"I feel warm and tingly," she said.

"You're experiencing the Great River of Life in and around everything," he told her.

He made a couple more passes and the muscles in her body relaxed. It was as if someone had tucked a warm blanket around her. His hands paused a few inches above her naval. "It feels like you're pulling something out of me," she said.

"In a way, I am," he acknowledged. "The solar plexus chakra is compromised and that severely limits the flow to your personal power. Without this energy, your self-esteem plummets and you won't have an accurate perception of who you are."

Eugene moved his hands in a small circle, and warmth spread through Clare's abdomen. After a minute, he moved directly above her heart. At first she didn't feel much, other than a slight twinge inside her chest, but pressure soon mounted and it felt like a pillar of cement was crushing her heart. She wriggled, uncomfortable. "What are you doing? That hurts."

Eugene adjusted his hands and a burst of heat pulsed through her. She swore each cell was blazing through her body like a flaming, out-of-control roller coaster. Terrifying, yet thrilling. She could not stop shaking. "What's happening to me?"

The medicine man put a reassuring hand on her shoulder. "The Life Force is moving through you, clearing blocks. Close your eyes and take a deep breath."

Clare did as she was told, and had the oddest sensation of floating. Feeling for the table, she was consoled by the solidness beneath her, and squelched the urge to open her eyes.

Taking another deep breath, indescribably beautiful colors paraded within her mind's eye, more vivid than anything she'd seen. Stunning reds and oranges; yellows flowed into greens. Blues and purples bled into golden rays so brilliant, it was as if she were staring at a blinding river of color ten times brighter than the sun.

She was so relaxed, her bones were like rubber. Far in the distance, she heard a distorted voice tell her to breathe. Yes, breathing was good. She should breathe.

Another deep breath and she was gone.

Chapter Eight

RANSOM tinkered on the broken-down ATV, replacing a faulty spark plug with a new one he bought at the hardware store in town. Removing the fuel line from the carburetor, he held the line over an old coffee can checking the gas flow. Hmm. Sluggish. He blew through the line and checked again, gratified to see the fuel running freely.

The real test came when he turned the key in the ignition and the ATV growled to life. Satisfied, he cut the engine and was about to have a look at the rear axle when the medicine man and his dog emerged from the healing center.

The old man's leathered face lit at the sight of Ransom. "Wondered when you'd show. Felt the energy surge a week ago."

Before Ransom could answer, the monstrous dog lunged, knocking him a step backward, the huge front paws heavy on his shoulders. With tail wagging fiercely, the dog lavishly licked Ransom's face. Laughing, he scrubbed Roger's head. "It's good to see you too, big fella." This earned him another round of slobbery affection. God, if everyone could be a dog.

Eugene ordered the animal away and pulled Ransom into a friendly hug, giving him an enthusiastic clap on the back. With some sadness, Ransom noticed his long-time friend had lost a lot of weight, and looked frail. But he knew better than to ask the old healer questions to answers he knew.

Eugene lit a cigarette and gave Ransom the once over. "Got a new look, I see."

When they last met, Ransom had been taller and thicker, with curly hair and deep brown skin. Only his eyes remained the same.

"What are you calling yourself these days?" Eugene asked.

"Ransom Mayes."

The medicine man took a slow drag on the cigarette, working the name around in his head. "Ah, God's shield," he said with approval. He threw a thumb at the building behind him. "She got any idea who she's traveling with?"

"No. She doesn't know who *she* is."

Eugene grunted. "Hardly surprising. Her whole system was blown. Had to do a mind cleanse with a full chakra reboot. She's out cold sleeping it off."

Ransom met the old man's eyes, gratitude swelling in his chest. "I appreciate what you've done for her. Thank you."

"She's not out of the woods yet. These things take time and you don't have it. She's drawing them like a goddamn magnet. Have you told her?"

Ransom shook his head no. He didn't want to scare her. "How far back are they?"

Squinting at the sky, Eugene flicked away the cigarette. "Best guess? Two hours."

This confirmed Ransom's intuition. Whenever he tuned into the energy field, he felt a crippling wave of cold closing in on them.

"You hear about the cancer doctor in Florida?" Eugene asked. "Found him shot in his own home. Made it look like a goddamn robbery. That's three healers dead in the past six months, and two more are missing."

Ransom fell silent toeing the ground. He knew of the energy workers, and as much as it pained him, he couldn't intervene. The first rule had not been met. Someone must ask for his services before he could help. What a shame so many miracles were wasted because no one thought to ask for them.

His old friend laid a hand on his shoulder, a sympathetic look in his eyes. "Hey, no one blames you for what happened. We do what we can. Besides, you've got your hands full with her. And I've got to say, she's plenty strong-minded."

Strong-minded, thought Ransom, if only! There were times he found her downright pigheaded. The powerful ones were, he reminded himself. And Clare was indeed powerful.

The muscles in Ransom's jaw tightened when he thought of the risk he'd taken by bringing her here. Things could get ugly and his friend was not the robust man he once was. He said to him, "When they come for her, they'll find your healing center. You and your family might want to leave for a few days."

Eugene waved him off. "My work doesn't interest them. Shit, I'm barely a blip on their radar. She's the one that frightens them. Where will you take her?"

"I thought I'd go north."

"To the lake?"

Ransom nodded.

Eugene looked thoughtful. "Gitchi-gami has enormous energy. It'll slow those bastards while you figure out how to keep her safe."

"Slow whom?" Clare asked, stifling a yawn as she came around the corner surprising both men. Spying Ransom, her expression turned venomous. "Did you have a nice ride?" she asked through gritted teeth.

He did a so-so gesture. "Suspension feels mushy. Bet the pothole I hit knocked something out of alignment."

Fury rose in her face. He tried his best not to smile and failed. Aggravating her was entirely too much fun.

Clare unleashed her scowl on Eugene. "Who needs to be kept safe?"

"Not my news to tell," the old man said, and lit another cigarette.

Exasperated with the runaround, Clare narrowed her eyes on Ransom. "Either you tell me what's going on, or have fun walking home."

Ransom saw the old healer's face crease into a wide grin. He supposed there was some humor in the suggestion of him walking home, considering his home was nowhere Clare could imagine.

"Well?" she said waiting, arms stiffly crossed over her chest.

Maybe this was the time to reveal her path. He'd been waiting for such a moment. How she took what he had to tell her was anyone's guess. Hopefully, she'd listen to him. Her life depended on it.

Looking her in the eyes, his throat was strangely dry. He said, "We're being followed by men who've been hired to find you."

At first, Clare simply stared at him. In her wildest dreams, Ransom knew she would not have fathomed such a thing. She stole a look at Eugene, his face grim. Her eyes slid back to Ransom, and her voice wavered.

"What are you talking about?"

Ransom said, "You have the potential to become a powerful healer, and that frightens people."

Clare blinked, and then her lips curled into a smile. "Wow. You had me going."

"I'm telling the truth."

Annoyance replaced her smile. "What people?"

"There are those who view your gift as an obstruction to their bottom line."

"An obstruction?" Eugene snorted, and pointed his cigarette at her. "They want you dead."

Clare tensed. She shook her head trying to make sense of what she was hearing. "This is crazy. You're both crazy. I can't even take care of a plant. Why would anyone want me dead?"

Before Ransom could answer, Eugene jumped in. "Woman, you have the power to bring healing peace to the world. How popular do you think you are with those profiting off people's misery? Big money in misery." He looked at Ransom. "Tell her. She's a goddamn miracle worker."

Clare turned panic-filled eyes on Ransom, and he felt her energy plummet. Not happy, he faced his friend. "This might go better if I talk to Clare alone."

It took a minute for Eugene to catch Ransom's drift, but when he saw the fear on Clare's face, the old healer shrugged apologetically. "Guess I'll go see what the wife's doing."

He headed for the house. The dog trotted beside him, nose tracking the ground.

Slowly inching away from Ransom, Clare's eyes darted to her car, ready to bolt. He took a cautious step toward her. "Stay away from me," she warned.

Ransom froze in place. Calmly, he said, "You're in danger, but I'll do my best to protect you."

"*Protect me?* You're scaring the hell out of me. I'll feel safer when I get away from you."

She stepped past him and Ransom caught her hand. "You want to tell me the reason you wear long sleeves?" he asked.

Her eyes narrowed. "Let go."

But Ransom didn't let go. Pushing back her sleeve, he exposed a jagged scar across her wrist. Just looking at it was like a stab to his heart. He said, "You bought the razor blades at a hardware store you saw on your way home from work."

A horrified gasp left Clare's throat, and she quit struggling.

"In line, the lady in front of you carried a small child in her arms, a curly-haired toddler who giggled and reached for you. Your heart was so heavy, you stepped into a different line."

She looked away, eyes watering. "I don't remember."

Ransom nodded, she remembered. He knew she would. The child was an especially painful reminder of her growing despair. "The clerk tried to flirt with you and forgot to give you your change. You remembered at the exit and decided not to go back. Pointless, you thought. Soon you'd have no need for money."

She shook her head, stunned. "How do you know this?"

"I was with you," Ransom said quietly, and her eyes grew large. "You dropped the package and for a split second thought to leave it, but an elderly gentleman picked it off the floor handing it to you. He wished you a 'good afternoon.'" Ransom tenderly traced the scar with his finger. "And I was with you two nights later when you got into the bathtub and pressed the blade to this wrist."

"Impossible," she whispered squeezing her eyes shut. Tears tracked her cheeks. "I was alone."

"You're never alone. I'm always with you."

Recoiling, she pulled her hand from his grasp. "You're reading my mind."

"No."

"Then how do you know? Who are you?"

"Your guardian assigned to you at birth."

"Assigned to me? By whom?"

He looked at her intently. "God."

Clare's eyes narrowed. "You're lying."

"I don't lie."

"God's a concept people use to get others to do what they want. I don't believe in a being with the power to send someone to heaven or hell."

"Good for you," he said. "Don't believe it. Better yet, don't have any beliefs. Keep your mind blank like a sheet of white paper."

She frowned. "What are you talking about?"

"Beliefs are a form of judgment about how something has to be. What new inspiration can enter a mind that thinks it knows everything?"

Shifting her weight from one foot to the other, she surveyed him with a doubtful eye. "You're saying God sent you—no, *assigned* you to me. And you're what? A guardian angel? Where are your wings?"

"You're judging again. My job is to protect and guide you."

She folded her arms. "Why on earth would anyone be after me? I dress mannequins for a living. Or I did until this morning, no thanks to you. How do I know you're not scamming me?"

"For what reason?"

"Money."

He smiled. "You have less than two hundred dollars in your checking account, and your credit cards are maxed."

Incredulous, she pointed at him. "There. How do you know that?"

"I told you. I'm always with you."

"I've never seen you before."

He shrugged. "I don't show myself often, but you have felt me."

"When?" She stared.

He looked to her wrist. "What made you stop cutting yourself that night?"

Remembrance flashed across Clare's face, her expression softened. "A butterfly flew through my window. Strange, because they don't fly at night. It must have been drawn to the bathroom light."

She rubbed at the scar on her wrist. "The thing landed on my hand, the one with the razor blade, and sat there staring at me with those black eyes. I can't explain it, but killing myself in front of a butterfly didn't seem right." Her eyes suddenly widened. "That was you?"

He chuckled softly. "Do I look like a butterfly?"

Her chin dropped. "You're laughing at me."

"Clare, no. I asked for a miracle that night, because

my messages weren't getting through to you. In floated your butterfly."

"What messages?"

"How much you're loved. I sent songs through your radio urging you to 'stop in the name of love'. But when you're in the cold, empty space, the loud one has your ear and you can't hear anything else."

"The 'loud one'? Who's that?"

"It's the incessant, bossy chatter in nearly everyone's mind."

She tilted her head. "What do you mean?"

"When you're angry at someone, have you noticed a voice inside your head rallying you, building your sense of righteous indignation, rewinding conversations playing out scenarios where *they* get *theirs*."

"That's what you call the *loud one*?"

"It is. Left unchecked, the loud one can keep you in an agitated state for hours, maybe days, or longer."

Clare thought about this. "I guess I have been that angry, but it's not a special voice. It's just me."

"It's not you," Ransom said. "The natural you vibrates at a high rate of energy, and you feel deeply peaceful no matter what's going on in your life. In contrast, how do you feel when you're angry?"

Clare shoved her hands inside her pockets. "This is stupid. Everyone gets angry. It's normal."

"Normal, yes. Natural, no. Anger is part of a low energy system and is extremely harmful to your body. Fear is at its core. The loud one voices fear inside your mind by forever complaining and judging. Nothing's ever good enough. *You* aren't good enough. Fear is a denial of the truth of your being." Ransom stared at Clare. "The night I couldn't get through to you, what were you thinking?"

Clare's gaze shifted to the ground, her voice cracked with emotion. "I wanted to end the pain. I still do. My therapist gave me a prescription, but I can't snap out of whatever this is. I'm such a mess."

"Clare, look at me," Ransom said. She lifted her eyes to his. "You're in the dark night of the soul, an intense suffering different than grief. It's different than depression caused by things like hating your job. The dark night brings heightened awareness of your innermost feelings cleansing your deepest fears. You notice what you refused to before."

Her voice dropped. "The sadness is so heavy, I feel like I'm wearing it."

He nodded, knowingly. "Many spiritual people have gone through this journey. Once through, your sense of peace is unshakable."

Hugging her shoulders, she let out a long stuttered breath. "A year ago I had the man of my dreams. We would've been married by now, but I blew it."

"Why do you say that?"

"He wanted children, and I didn't. It was a deal breaker." She shook her head. "I don't get it. I like kids. I do. Except I know I'd seriously screw them up if they were mine. My stomach hurts talking about it."

"Why is that?"

Her jaw quivered. She dug in her pocket for a Kleenex. "I can't imagine. My parents are wonderful. I had a great childhood. There's no reason for me to wig out over this. My ex-fiancé tried to convince me I'd feel differently about our own children."

"Might you?"

"I wish!"

"If you could change your feelings, would he come back?"

She dabbed at her eyes. "He's moved on."

Ransom's tone was gentle. "If there's nothing you can do to change how things are, you must accept the circumstance and your feelings of sadness."

Her jaw clenched. "How am I supposed to do that? I've been trying."

"Suffering is caused by the idea something should be different than what it is. Ask for the help you need and watch for your signs. Something, or someone, will come along at the perfect time." He patted his chest and grinned. "Like me."

Clare managed a weak smile. "Then I'm in trouble, because my life's been chaos since I met you."

The medicine man walked out of his house, the dog led the way. His expression was dire. "Energy's been dropping. Be smart to get on your way."

Ransom agreed. The energy was heavy. They were coming.

Eugene handed him a brown paper sack. "The wife packed food."

Grateful, Ransom accepted the package and turned to Clare. "Time to go."

She dug in her heels. "Not until I know what's going on. You said I'm in danger because I'm a powerful healer?"

"I said you have the *potential* to be a healer—once you're trained. We need to drive to Lake Superior. The lake's higher energy will protect you and advance your skills at a faster rate."

Abruptly, the dog's ears laid back and he tucked his tail. Lips thinning, a low growl erupted from his throat. Eugene winced, shaking out his hands. "Damn. Pins and needles."

Ransom knew Clare wasn't strong enough to resist the men who followed them. Not yet. He had to convince her to leave. He took her by the shoulders and looked directly into her eyes. "I'd die before letting anyone hurt you. Do you trust me?"

She swallowed hard. "I think so."

"Then please, Clare, can we go?"

Chapter Nine

THE moment Clare pulled into the Hayward gas station, Ransom went on hyper-alert. He wouldn't let her out of the car until he'd scanned every person entering or leaving the store.

"You're freaking me out," she told him.

"Won't be the last time," he said, pulling money from his wallet. "I'll pump while you pay."

She objected. "I have money. I don't need yours."

Ransom raised his brows. "Remember, I know what's in your bank account."

Rather than argue, she gave him a serious eye roll and tucked the bills into her purse. "You want anything?"

"Water. And don't be gone long," he warned. He got out to pump gas.

"Don't be gone long," she mimicked. He was such a giant pain.

Inside the store, she found herself searching every face trying to decide if they were out to get her. Someone behind her opened a can of soda, and she jumped a foot. She turned around and glared at the guy for no reason. Jeez, Ransom had her acting half nuts.

Pull it together, she told herself, and quickly finished her shopping. She bought chips, candy bars, and an energy drink for herself and a bottle of water for Mr. Crazy.

Ransom was halfway across the lot by the time she exited the store. He scowled when he saw her. "Relax, warden," she told him. "Haven't chewed through my chains, yet."

"That's a load off," he grumbled, grabbing the bag she carried.

He wasted no time escorting her back to the car, and held the door for her. Sliding behind the wheel, Clare glanced into those green eyes of his and was again struck by their perfect clarity. It was like staring into the depth of a clear lake and seeing a whole other world. Maybe he was her guardian. Was that possible? How else could he have known her darkest secrets?

Adjusting her side mirror, she watched him pull the water from the bag and toss the rest into the trash. She sucked in a sharp breath. What was he doing?

"Hey," she said, as he got in beside her. "That was my food."

"It's not food."

"It's what I eat."

"Not anymore."

Buckling, he twisted open the water and took a long drink while Clare fumed. He looked over at her expectantly. "Why aren't you driving?"

"I barely slept last night and I've got a splitting headache. I need *caffeine*—the caffeine you threw away without asking me."

"You mean the poison you were about to drink?"

"You're being ridiculous. It's got vitamins. Besides, the medicine man smokes cigarettes. That's healthy?"

Ransom stiffened and spoke with surprising sharpness. "Don't judge the decisions of others. You can't know what they're going through." He gave her an apple from the bag the medicine man's wife packed. "Eat this. The sugar gives the body a natural boost."

An apple? He had to be joking. "So it's perfectly fine for other people to do whatever they want, but I can't have a little caffeine?"

Ransom looked at her like she was the most insensitive person on the planet. "Eugene was sprayed with Agent Orange during his tour in Viet Nam. He has cancer. Cigarettes soothe him."

Wow. She sank against the seat. Who would've guessed? The man seemed downright feisty. She looked at Ransom. "I'm sorry. I didn't know. Can you fix him?"

His eyebrows rose. "What makes you think there's anything to fix?"

"You said he has cancer, right? Or don't guardians do those types of things?"

Ransom gave her a pointed look. "Don't assume a person isn't whole because of a disease. Eugene does have pain, but he isn't suffering."

"What's the difference?" she asked.

"Suffering comes from a mind obsessed by what should or shouldn't be happening. Eugene's mind is without chatter. He might have cancer, but he's aligned in body, mind, and spirit with the Creative Force. He's living in the present moment without the illusions of past memories or a future that never arrives."

Clare stared at him in disbelief. "You're a spaz, you know that? You want me to eat the apple?" She took a huge bite. The juice ran off her chin as she chewed. "Mmm, good. Won't do a thing for this headache blurring my vision, but hey, I'll drive with one eye closed."

She turned the key in the ignition, and Ransom leaned toward her touching her temple with one finger. Her breath caught. A current of warmth flooded every cell in her body relieving the awful pain in her head. She felt lighter, her posture straight and effortless. Brilliant gold light bathed everything she looked at—the steering wheel, her hands on the steering wheel, even the apple in her hand was glowing. Her entire body pulsed with this light.

She turned toward Ransom and had to shield her eyes from the brilliant explosion in the seat beside her. It was like sitting next to blinding bursts of shimmering rays, spiking in every direction. She froze. What was happening? She'd barely had the thought when the light faded and everything returned to normal, everything except for the bright gleam in Ransom's eyes.

Staring into those eyes, she cleared her throat. "I assume there's an explanation."

"Energy," he said.

"Seriously? That's your story? Energy?"

He cracked a wide smile. "What else could it be?"

She peered at him, poking him with a cautious finger, and he laughed out loud. Jerk. But how could she explain the light show or her cured headache?

Blowing out a breath, she shifted into drive, hoping she wouldn't regret her next question. "Where to next?"

"Amnicon Falls. You'll love it."

d

Amnicon Falls was roughly ten miles from the port city of Superior, Wisconsin. To get there, Clare drove north for an hour through wooded marshland. She kept sneaking sideway glances at Ransom wondering if an angelic being would stuff half a sandwich in his mouth and belch like a rhino? Yet she could think of no rational explanation for the soothing warmth she felt at the exact spot where he'd touched her. Ransom Mayes was a real mystery.

She cleared her throat. "I've never been to Amnicon Falls. Why do you want to go there?"

Concentrating on her phone's GPS, he answered without looking at her. "Beautiful place to stretch the legs."

Stretching the legs sounded good to Clare. She was ready to get out of the car. Following his directions, she turned onto a county highway. The entrance was less than a quarter mile further.

Ransom bought a day pass at the park station, and she drove to an empty lot near an island trailhead. Getting out of the car, Clare was struck by the startling beauty. The previous evening's snowfall clung to every surface, dusting trees and layering the ground in pristine white.

She looked around, breathing in the crisp air, and an unexpected lift penetrated her usual depressed mood. "This place is incredible."

Ransom gave her a told-you-so smirk. Seeming in high spirits himself, he took her arm and said, "Come on, let's walk."

They followed a split-rail fence that zigzagged along the river, and were led to a covered bridge. Their boots scraped against rugged planks as they walked to the bridge railing admiring the view.

The Amnicon River snaked a dark course through the rocky gorge, cascading over a series of ice-crusted ledges. Clare noticed the water was a peculiar rusty color, and the foam from the falls reminded her of a root beer float.

"Why do you suppose the water looks like this?" she asked Ransom.

"Not a clue," he said.

A deep voice answered from somewhere below them. "The color comes from roots and decaying vegetation leached from bogs in the area."

Staring at them through a camera lens was a man wearing winter camouflage gear and tall rubber boots. The man clicked off a rapid succession of shots before climbing up the snowy bank with ease. He joined them on the bridge and grinned. "Sorry, couldn't help butting in. Hope I didn't startle you guys."

"Nope," said Ransom, making their introductions. And for once he didn't mention the accident that brought them together. Small miracle, Clare thought.

The man shook hands with both of them. He had a firm, confident grip. Clare liked him immediately. "Kendrick Stephens," he said. "I'm one of the rangers here. It's my day off, but I wanted to take a few pictures for the park website while the snow's fresh."

The ranger did a quick scan of his photos, looking pleased. "Nice," he said, and turned the screen so Clare could see.

It was a picture of her and Ransom leaning over the railing. A halo of bright white light surrounded her head. Interestingly, there wasn't anything special around Ransom.

"How did you do this?" she asked the ranger.

"I didn't. The camera caught your aura."

"My aura?"

"It happens sometimes," he told her. "The surprise is the ones I don't see."

Clare shook her head. "Wait a minute. You see auras?"

He nodded. "Yep. I do."

"Can you see my aura?"

Stepping back a few feet, Kendrick studied her and frowned. "You've got some gray in your heart area."

"Is that bad?" He kind of looked like it was.

"In my experience, gray tends to signify a block in the energy flow. Since I see it over your heart, my guess is there's not much joy in your life. Usually the person is experiencing some kind of loss."

Clare was stunned. "How could you know?"

"The aura contains information about the essence of what it surrounds. I've noticed certain colors seem to reveal personality traits and emotions." Kendrick glanced above Clare's head. "I see glowing white light from your shoulders to the top of your head. This often means you're being guided and protected."

Ransom nudged her. "What was that about being guided?"

Kendrick half-laughed. "I know. Hokey, right? You guys probably think I'm nuts. I wouldn't have believed any of this either a couple years ago."

"What changed you?" Clare asked.

"Got struck by lightning."

"What? How?"

"I was fishing on a lake when I shouldn't have been. My heart rate shot to 186 beats per minute. Had to take medication for over a year to keep it regulated." He rubbed his fingertips together. "Fingers and toes are slightly numb, otherwise I'm good. My doctors are scratching their heads."

Clare was flabbergasted. "That's how you started seeing auras?"

He shook his head yes. "Once I saw the energy, I remembered I used to see it as a kid."

"Energy?" Ransom taunted. "Isn't that the term the New Age nutcases use when they're taking about some mythical force?"

Clare cringed at Ransom's rudeness, but Kendrick nodded his approval. "A healthy dose of skepticism is a good thing in my book. Experience informs our sense of reality."

"Exactly," said Ransom.

Kendrick considered a moment before answering him. "I think of the 'force,' as you say, as an energy field permeating everything. Scientific studies conclude energy vibrating at a specific rate creates matter."

"Matter? You mean the things we see?" Ransom asked.

"And things we don't see—oxygen, for instance." Kendrick motioned toward the view beyond the bridge. "People don't know they see energy everywhere, because it's disguised as trees and rocks and rivers and clouds. The substance that forms life—I call it the God essence— is everywhere and in everything, although scientists have yet to determine what the substance is."

Widening his stance, Ransom folded his arms. "If that's true, how come more of us don't notice? Do we have to be struck by lightning?"

"Wouldn't recommend it," Kendrick smiled. "If you'd like, I can teach you how to see the auric field. Won't take long. Couple minutes, as a rule."

Ransom's gaze shifted to Clare. "How about it, Clare?

Think you've got what it takes to see auras?"

She hesitated, torn. There was no doubt Ransom was trying to manipulate her. He'd probably been doing it from the second they met. He wanted her to learn this. She was positive that's why he'd brought her here. It would be a perfect time to stand her ground and head for the car. And as much as she wanted the satisfaction of wiping that know-it-all smirk off his face, she was equally intrigued. Was it possible for her to physically see energy?

She pushed past Ransom and lifted her chin. "We'd love to take you up on your offer," she told Kendrick.

The ranger had them face the water. Ransom stood by Clare's side looking doubtful. Kendrick instructed them to massage the center of their forehead with the palm of their hand to stimulate the brow chakra. Next, he had them focus on the pine tree nearest them. He said, "Let your eyes go soft and slightly out of focus, almost like daydreaming.

Clare was lost. "Don't look at the tree?"

"Not directly. Look at the space surrounding the tree. At first, the energy will appear like a transparent line a couple inches thick, similar to heat radiation on a hot day. Keep watching and you'll see glowing white light."

Gazing softly, all at once she saw a wavy, ether-type substance on either side of the tree. A few seconds later a white light, brighter than any Clare had seen, pulsed in waves from the trunk. "I see it! Now what?"

"Maintain a soft focus," Kendrick said, "and try looking around at other objects."

Clare slid her eyes to a nearby boulder and, to her surprise, saw much the same light around the entire form.

She extended her field of vision to include clumps of tall grass and other trees. Astonishingly, everything radiated the same wavy glow.

Excited, Clare shifted her gaze to a squirrel on a log nibbling a seed, and everything faded. "Oh, no! The light's gone." She looked at Kendrick. "What happened?"

"Perfectly natural when you're learning," he explained. "Try again."

Clare took her eyes out of focus, and this time she saw the same glowing light around the animal. She gazed at the horizon. The same light pulsed, radiating five feet into the sky, spreading over everything she looked at. "This is mind-blowing!"

Kendrick said, "Slowly outstretch your hand and spread your fingers, keeping the sky in the background. Focus your gaze in the same way around your fingers."

Clare saw bright wisps between her fingers, like smoky string connecting each one. Turning her hand, she let out a small gasp. In her palm was a ball of white light!

She turned to Ransom and found him beaming at her. "Did you see the energy?" she asked. "Isn't it amazing?"

"Yes, amazing." He gave her an uncharacteristic squeeze and she went dizzy with euphoria.

Kendrick squinted to the west. "The sun sets in about an hour. Do you have someplace to stay tonight? The Parker Horse Ranch is five miles from here. I've stayed there. Great energy."

Ransom smiled. "Sounds like a plan."

Clare wasn't so sure. When they left for Hayward that morning, she hadn't expected to be away from home more than a few hours. She was a homebody by nature, and admittedly why she was so easily deceived by her last boyfriend.

The memory of Keith with the other woman crushed in on her, squeezing her heart with the familiar crippling sadness. She looked at Ransom with his handsome boyish face, enthusiastically getting directions from Kendrick, and suddenly she couldn't see him as anything other than a college student. What was she thinking, staying overnight with a kid? And why would he want to spend the night with her?

An icy shudder went through her leaving her feeling weak and tired. She tapped Ransom's shoulder. "I want to go home."

Chapter Ten

RANSOM didn't say a word while Clare started the car. Nor did he say anything as she fiddled with the heat control or the seat belt or the rearview mirror. She wouldn't look at him. He could feel the fear in her vibration, and knew the trackers would too. They were expert at sensing low energy. By letting fear control her thoughts and emotions, Clare had unwittingly increased their danger.

Turning within, he visualized brilliant light being absorbed into every cell of his body. When he felt strong and empowered, with the vibration moving through him, he focused on surrounding Clare in the same light. He set his intention for the highest possible outcome. He would've liked more time to gently ease her into her life's purpose, but he didn't have it. For her safety, he had to get tougher.

"You've forgotten who you are," he told her.

Bristling, she tightened her scarf. "I know who I am. I'm the person who doesn't want to spend more time with you!"

He gave her his sternest look, and let some edge into his tone. "Not only have you forgotten who you are, you've forgotten who I am as well." He paused, letting his words sink in. "I am your guardian. I've been with you since before your birth. Whether you accept this or not doesn't change the truth."

Clare's eyes widened, her agitated fidgeting stopped. Good. He had her attention.

"You *are* God's thought in form. You have yet to realize this is true. Heaven and earth lay at your feet in perfect obedience to your whispers of thought. There's nothing that doesn't obey this law. Your thoughts move mountains, but you've no grasp of your power. You're like a child playing with fire."

She groaned. "You're making a big deal out of nothing. Who cares what I'm thinking? Doesn't mean anything."

He could feel his patience slipping. "Your thoughts and emotions create your perception of what is real *for you*," he told her.

"So what am I creating?"

"Pain mostly, and lots of struggle."

She stared at him as if he were an idiot. "When have I thought, 'Gosh, I wish my life was harder, and could I please have more pain'?"

"Not in those exact words," he acknowledged, "but you have fantasized about horrible things happening to your boss. And you do blame your ex-boyfriend for how awful you feel."

"Well, yeah, but I was nice to them and they screwed me over. They're bad people. *They* caused me pain."

Ransom shook his head. She had no idea what was good or bad. "You judge everything based on *your* perception, which is clouded by anger and betrayal. These low-vibrating energies go out into the world as your thoughts and cling to other thoughts, magnifying the energy that created it. Since you must own what is yours, the low-vibrating energy you sent out, returns greatly enhanced.

"Remember, Clare, you give from what you have. If

you have pain, you will give pain, increasing your suffering. You can't escape the guiding rules of this planet."

She lowered her eyes, lip trembling. His words had struck a nerve. "You're not very comforting," she murmured.

"I didn't come for your comfort. I'm here to help you get so uncomfortable, you evict the *loud one* who holds your attention. No answers are found in a mind that wants death."

She blew into a tissue. "You act like everything's my fault."

He softened. "What is it you want, Clare?"

"I'm sick of feeling like this. I don't care about anything anymore. There are days I can barely get out of bed. I'm exhausted. Everything hurts."

Ransom nodded. "It's excruciating to go against what's natural, and exceptionally easy to stay in the flow of life."

She was incredulous. "How can you say it's easy? I haven't noticed many enlightened people on the news lately."

"With each breath you take, do you consciously instruct the lungs on how to do their job?"

"Well, no. I take it for granted."

"This is what your natural state is like; effortless, and maintained perfectly without thought. Sustaining the mental perception takes herculean effort. Every aspect of your life suffers—your health, wealth, relationships, and your sense of well-being. You surrender everything naturally yours to keep a painful lie."

She considered a moment. "Why is it hard to be natural?"

"Because you don't remember who you are and what your natural state is. You're listening to the wrong voice."

Hands in the air, she let out a frustrated groan. "You're talking in circles. I give up!"

Finally! Ransom pounded the dash, making her jump. "That's the first sane choice you've made. Give up thinking you know anything. Give up thinking altogether. *No thinking.* Keep one thought in your mind: *I do not know.*"

She frowned. "Why would I not want to think?"

"The part of you who wants to 'get out of pain' is the part of you who decided for pain and doesn't know it. This misguided mental perception of you looks at the pain and acts shocked. "Not mine," it says. This pain is a mystery and shouldn't be here, yet it thinks about nothing else. It will analyze, question, blame, complain, judge, and attack the pain. It does everything but thank and love what it has created. This is your unconscious habit.

"Decide this one thing—to freely and lovingly embrace with gratitude whatever pains you, then don't give it another thought."

Shifting in her seat, Clare looked less than convinced. "How can I love pain? That seems wrong. And how can I quit thinking about something that's hurting me?"

These were good questions. He was impressed. "Have you noticed how a child drops a toy when they've finished playing with it? They let the toy fall from their hands without looking back, completely withdrawing their attention."

She nodded. "I've seen kids do that."

"Okay. For the child who has *outgrown* the toy, the temptation to play with it is gone as well. They instinctively know the experience no longer serves them. The toy can be in front of them, but it ceases to exist as an option. The child easily turns from the toy and walks away."

She shook her head, brows knitted in confusion. "Are you saying we have to do the same thing with our pain?"

"Do the same with *everything* in your life. Love your experiences by saying *yes* to everything that shows up. Accept everything, knowing at some level you've created the experience for your higher understanding or it wouldn't be there. If there is pain, listen to what it tells you, but don't fear it. Fear makes the pain larger because what you put your attention on increases. Look at the experience for what it is, and love it as *yours*. This is the way out of suffering.

"Give thanks with your whole heart for your creative powers for they allow you an 'out.' If you don't particularly enjoy what you're experiencing, withdraw your attention, like the child drops the toy, with the firm understanding the Source of All is *with* you, never against you."

Clare's eyes danced with excitement. "I think I'm getting this! I've been fighting against what's created and causing myself more pain. What I need to remember is everything in my life is something *I've* created, and honor the experience as proof of the creative force inside me. Knowing this helps change my perception and allows the opportunity for change, because I won't be feeding the creation with more low-vibrating thoughts."

"You've got it." Ransom beamed, sensing a higher shift in her energy. She was doing great.

Clare looked like she was feeling good about things herself, she practically glowed. "Uh, about this horse ranch," she said tentatively. "You did get the directions?"

He pretended to be shocked. "Why, Clare Davis, I thought you didn't want to spend any more time with me."

She flashed him a wicked grin that had his heart tripping over itself. "Guess I can put up with you a little while longer."

Chapter Eleven

BLONDE dynamite was Clare's impression of Shannon Parker, the petite ranch owner who welcomed them into her home—tiny, but strong, with a calloused handshake and a megawatt smile. She was dressed for the barn in a flannel shirt and jeans, and smelled faintly of horse and hay.

The second-generation Parker home was a two-story white farmhouse with nine-foot ceilings and a large front porch. Shannon gave them a quick tour. Clare admired the maple floors throughout, and fell in love with the homey kitchen with its wood-burning fireplace.

An open staircase gave access to three bedrooms and a full bath. Similarly decorated, both guest rooms had a carved antique bed covered with a patchwork quilt, a braided floor rug, and a comfy-looking chair in the corner. The view looked out onto a red horse barn and large corral. Beyond, Clare could see a fenced pasture and thick woods. She counted more than a dozen horses in the snowy pasture eating from a pair of round feeders.

Having explained their lack of luggage, Shannon graciously lent Clare a long t-shirt to sleep in, and gave Ransom a pair of her husband's sweats.

"Bathroom has a shower," Shannon told them. "Towels are in the closet, and there's a package of new toothbrushes in the vanity drawer."

"Sounds great," Ransom said. "Thanks."

Shannon walked past them to the stairs. "There's beef stew on the stove, help yourselves. One of the horses spooked and ran through the fence. Did a nasty job on his leg. My husband's at work, and the vet's in the barn. I've got to get back out there."

"Poor thing," said Clare. "We'll be fine. You go."

Shannon quickly descended the stairs. A few seconds later they heard a door slam and the house was quiet. Ransom sniffed the air. "Food smells good. Are you hungry?"

"Starved," said Clare. The hearty aroma made her stomach growl. She hadn't eaten anything except the apple Ransom had given her.

In the kitchen they found dishes in the cabinet and a loaf of homemade bread on the counter. Clare ladled the stew into bowls, and Ransom cut thick slabs of bread, slathering them in butter. Her mouth watered in anticipation.

They sat at the table. Clare was about to dig in when Ransom grabbed her hand, bowing his head in prayer. "Thanks for the food. We appreciate it."

He dropped her hand and stared at her, his tone serious. "Don't let an opportunity pass to express your gratitude. This important tool works like magic for attracting more of life's good things. More joy, more friends, more fun. Gratitude attracts *more*. Coupled with intention, it's unstoppable and creates reality as you desire to see it."

That sounded wonderful to Clare. Taking his hand, she bowed her head. "Thanks for Ransom Mayes... I think." She laughed. "Can we eat now?"

Ransom grabbed his spoon, a wide grin on his face. "See? A little gratitude and you're already more fun."

They made short work of the meal. The stew was delicious, and Clare was stuffed. After putting the bowls in the dishwasher, Ransom suggested they sit on the porch and let their stomachs settle.

Bundling into jackets, they headed outdoors. The cold air was invigorating after the warmth of the kitchen. They sat side by side on rockers facing a snowy field with rows of corn stubble. The field took on a rosy glow with the sinking sun.

Clare breathed deeply. She couldn't remember a time she'd been more content. "Wish I could stay here forever."

"It is nice," Ransom agreed.

Clare looked over at him while he soaked in the view. "I have a question. How come your aura didn't show on the ranger's camera?"

"I blocked the image," he said matter-of-fact.

"You can do that?"

He glanced at her, eyes playful. "Apparently. A conversation based on my energy wouldn't have been productive."

"Okay, smarty pants. If energy is everywhere and in everything, why don't I see it all the time?"

"You see what you believe you see. Change your mind and the scene changes. The outer world is a reflection of your inner thoughts and nothing more."

Clare could feel her cheeks grow hot. "Do you know how irritating you are? You think I enjoy having crappy things happen to me?"

"I've told you, you are God's thought in form. What that means is you are an independent, yet essential part of the prime moving force that creates your perception of reality by what you are thinking. If you want something different, make a choice for it and think of nothing else.

Trust everything you need, for your highest good exists within you."

"If I have everything I need, why don't I experience this in my life?"

Reaching out, Ransom touched the tip of Clare's nose, surprising her. "How often do you notice the nose on your face?"

"What's my nose got to do with anything?"

"Humor me," he said.

"Fine. I don't usually look at my nose."

"But you can see it whenever you want to?"

She nodded, impatiently drumming her fingers on the arm of the rocker, wondering his point.

"That's sort of how creation is—always there, but you aren't fully aware of it. When you look in a mirror and see your nose, is the image your real nose? Or is the image reflecting back to you what is currently taking place?"

"It's a reflection," she said.

"This is similar to what happens when you look outside yourself for answers. It's like looking in the mirror and expecting the image to have the solutions for your life. When you don't like what you see, you blame the image and fight against it. The reflection is nothing. It doesn't think, feel, hear, or see. If you want answers, look within and trust what you *feel*. Trust your guiding instincts."

"Ah, the old reflect within," Clare joked.

He broke into a smile. "Yes. As much as you are able, first look within and assess the quality of your thoughts. Drop the ones that don't match the life you desire, and see what the reflection shows."

He stopped rocking and leaned toward her cautioning, "Don't get attached to what you see. You'll want to label everything as good or bad. This is a mistake."

"Why?"

"Life is the creative force that allows every possible experience. Only a misguided mind would attempt to label what is limitless, essentially blocking its own natural limitless state. Act on the thoughts that come to you when your mind is without the noisy inner dialogue. These build your world without causing suffering."

Ransom spoke with an enviable confidence far beyond his years. Clare was struck by how charismatic he was when he wanted to be. There was something about Ransom Mayes that made her want to be near him.

Drawing her attention to the snow-crusted field, he asked, "What do you see?"

The sky was on fire with the setting sun. Clare's breath caught. "I don't know when I've seen a brighter red. It's spectacular."

"This is the red of the root chakra. The sun's red energy gives you a physical boost enhancing your will to live. Mentally see your root chakra spinning in a clockwise direction pulling in this light."

Clare imagined her root chakra whirling like a mini tornado. "Am I supposed to feel something?"

"You're holding your breath," he observed. "Breathe, and try again."

Taking a couple deep breaths, Clare noticed a tingle at the base of her spine. She took another few breaths concentrating on the energy, and the tingle moved higher. She felt herself blush. "This is embarrassing, but there's a lot of warmth in my lower belly."

Ransom didn't look surprised. "You're experiencing sacral chakra energy. See how the sky is turning from red to orange? With an open chakra, you're able to give and receive physical pleasure."

Rays of brilliant yellow pierced the orange, and the vibration moved to her midsection. She put a hand over the area above her naval and was astonished by the turning energy registering in her palm. "Is this my solar plexus chakra?"

"Yes. This is your personal identity within the universe."

Awestruck, Clare watched as the rest of the chakra colors briefly presented—green for heart energy, blue for the throat, and a deeper blue enhanced her inner knowing. Purple was the last color on the horizon. Breathing the color into her crown chakra, her body pulsed with so much energy she felt like she could run for miles without stopping.

"How are you feeling?" Ransom asked.

"Wonderful! Did you make the sun do that?"

"I did. Just for you."

"Really?"

"No." He chuckled. "The rising and setting of the sun is one of the ways you receive energy. Your entire being was nourished by this light. Light, Life, God. These words are interchangeable. Look beyond the five senses and notice how well life takes care of you."

Clare had to admit, she'd never felt this good.

"God is a living impulse that *is* everything, the visible and the invisible. Do you understand what I'm saying?"

She shook her head. "Not really."

Again, he motioned at the view. The last of the sun's light was nothing more than a faint ember. "Describe what you notice."

Clare let her gaze wander over the dusky landscape. "I see snow and corn stalks."

"What else?"

What else? She peered harder. "Shadows, I guess. Is that what you mean?"

"What else?" he asked.

She looked above her. "There's a sliver of moon and a few stars in the sky. Oh, and I see you and me, and the house and porch, and the rockers we're sitting on."

She was about to name more objects when Ransom stopped her.

"That's fine, Clare, but what about the space containing the things you see? The space is what allows you to notice everything else."

She fell silent. He was right. Without space, the brain wouldn't be able to differentiate between objects. This invisible field was huge in comparison to everything else, yet she hadn't paid any attention to it.

"This is what I mean by God is *everything*," he told her. "If you give your whole focus to the physical, you won't see much of God."

As Clare contemplated Ransom's words, a pitiful, high-pitched horse squeal broke the quiet. They both flinched. The horse screamed again. The poor animal was hurting and Clare wished there was something she could do.

She could feel Ransom's eyes on her. "Would you like to learn how to help him?"

Chapter Twelve

RANSOM followed Clare into the barn and was soothed by the comforting warmth and the quiet sounds of animals settling in for the night. Clare waved a hand in front of her nose. "Whew. We're in a barn alright."

Built on a limestone foundation, the refurbished building had a small tack room at the entrance, hay storage overhead, and a dozen box stalls running parallel to the center aisle. Once they got their bearings, Ransom gestured for Clare to lead the way to the injured horse.

She frowned. "How would I do that? I don't know where he is."

"By feeling the energy."

"Feel?" She looked even more confused.

Ransom put his hands on her shoulders and spun her outward, away from him. "Shut your eyes and bring your hands up, palms out, and tell me what you feel through them."

She did as he asked. A few seconds went by. "I don't know. Moving air?"

"Is the air warm or cold?"

"Breezy. Is a fan on?"

Ransom turned her toward one of the stalls. "Tell me what you feel."

"Warm. Tingly." She sounded surprised. "What does that mean?"

"What does the sensation mean to you? For instance, does this stall feel empty, or is there a horse inside?"

She hesitated, shook her head slightly. "I can't tell."

"Take a guess. You've got a fifty-fifty chance of getting it right."

After a minute, her shoulders tightened. "I think there's a horse inside."

She didn't sound overly confident. "Are you certain?" he asked.

Her hands dropped, and she faced him with a frustrated glare. "I can't do this. I don't know what I'm supposed to feel."

Ransom rubbed the back of his neck, his own irritation rising. Dense emotions were contagious, and in this human body he was not entirely immune to their effects. He knew he was pushing, but she *had* to get this. Understanding the energy system was Clare's only defense against the men who hunted her. If she could help the horse, she'd strengthen her ability, greatly increasing her chances.

He gathered his patience. "We could both use a break. How about trying a different technique to raise our energies?"

She looked cranky, but receptive. He instructed her to shake out her hands and bounce on her feet. He did the same. They swiveled their hips and rolled their heads from side to side. When she was smiling, her body loose, he had her take a few deep breaths and bring her attention inward to her heartbeat.

He said, "Feel your heart expand with each breath, filling your entire being with radiant, healing light."

Her face was serene. She said, "My whole body is vibrating."

Brilliant light surrounded Ransom. Inhaling deeply,

his energy soared. The intimate connection pulsed through him. Taking one more breath, he opened his eyes fully refreshed, every trace of irritation gone.

He clapped his hands sharply, and said, "Break's over. How do you feel?"

She beamed at him. "I bet I could find that horse now."

He turned her toward one of the stalls. "Prove it."

Familiar with the drill, she shut her eyes and reached out. "My palms feel warm and tingly."

He moved her over one stall. "How about now?"

Concentrating, her forehead creased. "I don't feel anything. There's a horse in the first stall, and not in this one."

"Correct." He gave her shoulders a reassuring squeeze. She was doing well. He turned her so she faced the length of the barn. "Where's the injured horse?"

She rocked in her stance getting comfortable, and blew out some air. Ransom felt her muscles relax. "He's on the end," she said with confidence.

"Right side or left?"

"The right. My hands feel like they're on fire."

Ransom led her to the back of the barn to the last stall on the right. They both peered through the bars. As Clare predicted, the black Quarter Horse was lying on his side panting. Shannon Parker held his massive head in her lap, and stroked his sweat-soaked neck. A neat line of stitching ran from his shoulder down to his bandaged knee.

The stallion's ears pricked at the sound of strangers in the doorway. Tail switching, he watched them with terrified eyes.

Shannon looked as much on edge as her horse. Her tone was protectively sharp. "Sorry, you can't be back here. Tuck's not ready for company."

"We know something about healing with energy," Ransom told her. "It might help with his pain."

Shannon gave Ransom a hard look, deciding what to do. As if on cue, the stallion jerked his head up and squealed in obvious distress. She nodded for them to enter. "Please, no sudden moves," she cautioned. "He might spook."

"Understood," Ransom said.

Easing back the door, Ransom motioned for Clare to follow him into the stall. She stayed tight on his heels, her hand at his back, and he could feel her apprehension. He knew the horse could too. The stallion followed their every move with wary eyes, while Shannon caressed him and spoke in a reassuring tone.

Holding the stallion's gaze, Ransom calmly worked his way toward him. "Hey there, big guy. Looks like you've gotten yourself into some trouble."

The horse snorted but stayed put, allowing Ransom to slowly drop to one knee. Holding out a hand for the stallion to smell, the animal pushed his muzzle into it. Ransom stroked him. "That's a good boy."

Without taking his attention from the horse, Ransom quietly reminded Clare to breathe, taking in energy. When he felt her vibration lift, he signaled for her to come closer.

Kneeling beside him, Clare whispered, "Now what?"

Reaching for her hands, he gently placed them on the horse's large chest. "By touching, you connect with

Tuck's energy field. Visualize sparkling Source Light entering your crown chakra, through your heart, and out your palms into the horse. With gratitude, ask the Creator for guidance for the highest good. Keep your mind blank without thoughts, and wait. You'll be led what to do next."

Nodding, Clare waited. She did her breathing and waited some more. Finally, she sat back on her heels, discouragement in her voice. "I must not be doing it right. My hands were prickly and buzzy before, but now—nothing. Shouldn't I feel *something*?"

"When you call on the Creator, you call on Full Power. What do you consider 'full power' to mean?" he asked her.

Her long lashes fluttered. "I don't know how this works. I'm just doing what you told me."

"Clare," he said softly. "There's no reality as 'a little bit.' It is *all* and it is *complete*. This is the way Source creates."

Her body sagged. "So it is me. What did I do wrong?"

"When you had your hands on Tuck's chest, what were you thinking?"

"I was hoping I could help him."

"Every time you put your hands on a living being, you enter a sacred bond with the Divine in you and the Divine in the other. If you allow your mind to wander, you've lost communication with the One Who Heals."

"Even if I wanted him to get better?"

"You were expecting results."

"Well, yeah. What's wrong with that?"

"The tiny misguided mind hoping for results doesn't

know the results. It's guessing. You heal as God when you let the Source of All work *through* you. There's no conflict because you're clear Source knows what it's doing. Your mind is quiet without thought while you wait."

She tilted her head. "What is it I'm waiting for?"

"You're waiting for the whisper that enters the silent mind, bringing the answer and filling you with peace."

Shannon frowned, puzzled. "Are you talking about the voice of God? How are you supposed to hear that?"

"You have to be alert and without thought, like you're listening for a tiger in the woods and your whole life depended on your ability to hear it. With this type of alert stillness, a brilliant light fills you. Every cell is energized and fully powered. You feel there is nothing you can't do. This is Presence."

Both women gaped at him. "If that's the case, I'm tiger food," Clare said. "I don't know if I can stop thinking."

"You and me both," agreed Shannon.

"It's not hard," he said. "The requirement is for you to set your intention for the highest good, and let Source do the work."

Clare frowned. "In other words, get out of the way."

"If a surgeon were operating on a brain, would you jump in and take over or would you merely observe?" he asked.

"Let's hope I'd observe, otherwise I wouldn't put much faith in the patient's recovery." Clare paused, thinking. She looked at Shannon, brows raised questioningly.

"I'd like to try again to help Tuck, if that's okay with you?"

Shannon nodded her approval.

Cautiously, Clare put her hands on the horse, his ears nervously twitched. And despite Shannon's attempts to soothe him, the big animal tried to rise. Swiftly, Ransom laid his hands over Clare's. The energy flowed into the horse, relaxing him back into Shannon's lap.

Clare's jaw clenched, and he could tell she was frustrated. "I feel the energy, but you're the one facilitating the healing and not me. I know you believe I'm a great healer, but I'm not."

"Healing is an experience, not a thought," he explained. "You're trying to figure out *how* the energy works. *How* to heal."

She shrugged. "What's wrong with that?"

"You have it backwards. Your mind functions similar to a computer, miraculous in its own way, but unable to create new data. Quiet the mind, and inspiration flows into you from Source."

"How! When one thought leaves, another takes its place?"

"Choose a word as a failsafe. When your mind unconsciously rambles, break the train of thought by calling to mind your word."

Clare hesitated. "Any word? I could use 'butterfly'?"

"Butterfly is an excellent word," he told her. He thought of the tiny creature that had floated into her bathroom. She had come close that night to ending her life, too close. Yes, butterfly was a wonderful word.

Shannon looked confused. "How does using a different word quiet the mind?"

"Your mind can't concentrate on two streams of thought simultaneously. If you focus on something different, the mind drops whatever else it was thinking. This provides the opening for your mind to drop all thought and go blank, like a white sheet of paper."

Clare drew back with a defeated sigh. "Now I'm thinking about white paper. This is maddening."

"It does take practice," he admitted. "Let the thoughts flow when they come, just don't let them carry you away."

Shannon said, "Someone told me thinking about a problem creates a worse problem."

"It creates the idea that there *is* a problem," he said. "We are asked to have no belief of how something *has to be*. In this way we move into alignment with *what is*. This is the space of Source, and Source does not have a problem. Source is the Answer. And its only answer is *yes*, no matter what you're thinking. Until you see only Source in its countless forms, *do not think*."

Shannon was unconvinced. "Tuck's x-rays show a fractured kneecap. If it doesn't heal, he could be lame. Are you telling me this isn't a problem?"

"Don't get caught in what you see," he warned. "What you see can change in an instant."

Taking hold of the women's hands, Ransom inhaled deeply, visualizing light permeating every cell of his being, lifting everything within his energy field. On his exhale, the women's bodies pulsed in high vibration.

He placed Clare's hand over the horse's injured shoulder and Shannon's hand on the horse's bandaged knee. He said, "Thank you Source for taking care of what I do not know. You are the love, light, and healing energy that flows through Tuck for his highest good."

A whoosh of current surged through Ransom and the women and out their palms, flooding the injured stallion with energy. The horse whinnied as the jagged tear vanished beneath the stitches. Both women stared in shocked silence.

The stallion rolled forward and sprang to his feet, and everyone got out of the way. He nuzzled Shannon, making low nickering sounds. Overjoyed with relief, she flung her arms around the horse. "Thank you," she said to both of them, tears filling her eyes. "Thank you, thank you, thank you."

Caught in the moment, Clare hugged Ransom. "That was incredible," she said.

He agreed. It was nice to see her so excited. And as powerful as the experience was, he knew they'd barely scratched the surface of what was possible for her.

Chapter Thirteen

THE next morning Clare woke with a start. The house was dark and quiet. The time on her cellphone read 6 am. She'd had the strangest dream. Everything about it was unlike anything she'd experienced. She couldn't wait to talk to Ransom about it. Odd how much she was growing to value his opinion.

Through her window she saw the horse barn, and her thoughts immediately turned to the big stallion and the surreal way his injury disappeared. Her palms felt normal this morning, but last night it was as if she were plugged into a lightning bolt. How was it possible for Ransom to heal the horse? Clare didn't know much about miracles, but that must have been one.

Dressing quickly, she tiptoed into the hallway. Shannon's bedroom door was closed. Ransom's door was wide open. Hmm. What would he look like asleep? Did guardians sleep?

Clare took a hesitant glance as she slipped by his room. The bed was made, the room empty. Come to think of it, she hadn't heard anything from his room the entire night. Could be while she slept, he floated off to Neverland. Or more likely he took her car again.

The thought had her heart beating faster as she hurried down the stairs. The smell of freshly brewed coffee drifted from the dimly lit kitchen, and she tensed when she didn't find him there. Would he really leave her? The idea was more disturbing than she wanted to admit.

Peering out the kitchen window, relief flooded her.

The Camry was in the drive where she'd parked yesterday. So where was he? The barn was dark, and he wasn't on the porch.

Putting on her coat to go look for him, she pulled her gloves from the pockets and a note from Ransom came with them. *Don't hog the coffee,* he'd written, and practically ordered her to meet him in the barn. She shook her head. Now that sounded like the warden.

Entering the barn with two travel mugs of coffee, Clare flipped on the light. Rows of fluorescents buzzed to life. Her breath hung in the air, and she heard the horses rustling in their stalls, blowing and snorting, waking to the new day.

Ransom was at the back of the barn closing the gate to Tuck's stall. On her approach, Ransom stretched and yawned and farted without apology. Straw clung to his matted hair and clothing. His pants zipper was open, and she was positive the horse smelled better. She'd never seen anyone in need of coffee more.

Ransom scratched at chin stubble and eagerly took the mug from her. He slurped the hot liquid as she peeked inside the stall. Tuck was on his side resting peacefully, eyes half closed, ears hanging back loosely. He nickered when he saw her, and Clare's heart melted.

"Morning boy," she said softly. "Looks like you're feeling better. Thank God for that."

"Amen," said Ransom automatically, his sleepy eyes working to focus.

Clare plucked a stray straw from his head. "You slept out here, didn't you? Were you worried about Tuck?"

He gave her that lopsided grin of his. "Is this the face of someone who's worried?"

She considered him. Even in his rumpled, smelly state, there was something appealing about him no matter what he did. He stifled another yawn. Yuck, it wasn't his breath. She decided it was the calm confidence in his clear green eyes. What she wouldn't give to have some of that unwavering certainty in her life.

"What makes you so sure of yourself?" she asked.

A gleam came to his eyes. "My superior intelligence."

Her eyes cut to his pants. "Your zipper's open, smart guy."

Laughing, he zipped up and grabbed her. Tucking her head under his arm, he mussed her hair like her older brother used to do when she was a kid.

"Hey, cut it out." She smoothed her hair back into place. "What are you, ten years old?"

"Not even close," he smirked, counting on his fingers. "Let's see. I was created before the earth... Add 4.5 billion, carry the one...." Wide-eyed, he whistled under his breath. "Wow. I'm older than dirt."

She couldn't help rolling her eyes. Ransom was obviously one of those annoying morning persons who woke to sunshiny days with a bird chirping on his shoulder.

"Come on, lighten up," he told her, giving her a soft chuck under the chin. She wanted to slug him.

Grabbing a blanket off Tuck's door, he startled her by putting an arm around her shoulders. He said, "Let's watch the sunrise. Get you pumped for the day."

"Rah," she said.

She trudged alongside him, letting him steer her out the back door to a loose mound of grassy hay. He flopped onto it and dragged her down next to him. The hay was soft, the air crisp. Diamond-shaped stars lit the black sky. They seemed close enough for Clare to touch.

Ransom covered their legs with the blanket. "Comfortable?" he asked her.

Nodding, she sipped her coffee and stole a glance at him. Head back, resting against the old barn wall, Ransom gazed at the sky, pure wonder on his face. If possible, he looked even younger to her.

"This view amazes me." His voice held a hushed reverence. "The ever-expanding force that created whole universes from wisps of its mind is the same power inside you and me. The vastness of creation is mind-blowing."

Clare happened to be thinking about just that. Pulling at a loose thread in the blanket, she cleared her throat. "I had a dream last night…"

Or was it a dream? How could she explain something so bizarre?

From the corner of her eye she saw him watching her. He took her hand, his grip warm and reassuring. "It's okay. You can tell me anything."

With his encouragement, she continued. "You know how you were talking about the vastness of space?"

"Uh-huh."

"Well, I think that same non-ending space is inside us."

There was an eagerness about him. "Go on."

"In my dream I went to a place where everything was black, but I knew the space was inside me. Like I was traveling deep inside of *me*."

She paused, trying to find the words to describe what seemed so real to her. "I was on the edge of this space, terrified to go further, until I heard a voice tell me not to be afraid. I rushed into black nothingness, and I could *feel* it was alive."

Clare looked at Ransom gauging his reaction. Did he think her crazy? But she read excitement in his expression. He nodded for her to continue.

"This nothing, yet living space contained my every desire, and I knew everything I needed was inside me. I floated there at peace, soaking in the aliveness." She gave him a cautious smile. "Nuts, right?"

His eyebrows rose with an expression of awe. For the first time he didn't look at her like a bowl of lint had more intelligence. It was unnerving. He said, "You experienced the womb of creation where physicality exists as pure energy."

She gave him a blank stare. What was he talking about?

Ransom's enthusiasm kicked into high gear. "Don't you see? Through your thoughts the unmanifested energy expresses as matter. You choose what matters for you!"

"Yes. That's how it felt to me. Nothing compares to the aliveness of this space, and it's inside me?"

"It *is* you. This unmanifested place is where the Creator and created merge as one without the illusion of separation. In this space the essence of everything exists, and it's 'there' whether you choose it or not. It simply *is*." He broke into a huge smile. "Tell me, Clare, knowing you had no needs, what did you choose?"

"I didn't choose."

He nodded. "Do you see what a gift your physical life is? It allows the concept you need *something*, which leads to choice in the matter."

It was ingenious, Clare had to admit. Yet something

about this seemingly perfect setup was bothering her. "Wouldn't we avoid a lot of pain and confusion if we stayed in the place where we didn't need anything?"

"No doubt, but you'd be missing the other half of God—*experience*. In the womb of unmanifested creation the thought of creating what you already have doesn't occur. It's sort of like having a book in your hand and making a choice to have a book in your hand. Why would you choose what you have?"

Ah, she might be getting this. She said, "In other words, I'd know Source, but wouldn't experience Source."

"Which would be unfortunate," he said. "Source experience is an enormous rush. It's another reason I'm here." He wiggled his eyebrows at her.

Clare laughed. What a lunatic. But she wasn't letting him off the hook that easy. "Okay, experiencing God might be fun for you, but my life isn't so great. Seems like anything that can go wrong, does."

"Because you don't remember who you are and why you're having a physical life."

She folded her arms. "I'm listening."

"You were fashioned *from* the Creator, *by* the Creator. There's nothing else you could be made from, and no one else could've made you, because there isn't anything else. In your purest unmanifested condition, you unequivocally know this, but don't experience this. You take it for granted that there's nothing but the awesome stuff you're made from."

"This existence sounds boring," Clare said. "That's not how I experienced it in my dream."

"True, yet you realized you weren't making a choice,

and instinctively knew there was more than the space you were floating in."

He was right. She did know.

"You choose to come out of the space to *experience* what you know. You create by *being* what you wish to create. You are *that* for whatever length of *time* you wish. When the creation no longer serves you, withdraw your attention and create something else by being what you create. *You* have full power to *be* whatever you choose."

Clare shook her head. "My life isn't this way. I can't be whatever I choose."

"Your life is exactly this way and so is everyone else's. God doesn't play favorites."

Clare could feel herself getting frustrated again. "I don't get it. What you're saying doesn't make sense to me."

"If you're *being* grumpy," he bumped shoulders with her, eyes twinkling, "you *experience* yourself as grumpy by attracting that energy to you so you have something to be grumpy about. If you're *being* happy, you *experience* yourself as happy by attracting that energy to you so you have something to be happy about. How much more enjoyable would your life be if you paid attention to what you're creating?"

Holy cow. This was big. "That's why you're on my case about not thinking," she said. "But now I'm scared to think!"

"Or, you could cut yourself a break," he told her. "A child learns how to ride a bike before they drive a car. You'll get the hang of it. I have faith in you." He looked like he meant it.

A lump formed in Clare's throat. Gratitude for Ransom welled inside her. She'd struggled for so long, and it felt good to be with him.

Linking her arm in his, she laid her head on his shoulder and they watched morning's first blush edge the horizon. Her energy rose as the seven chakra colors presented in distinct layers like the previous evening. How had she not noticed the phenomenon before? What else hadn't she noticed?

Chapter Fourteen

CLARE watched the sunrise with Ransom, and for the first time in her life she didn't feel alone until a troubling thought occurred. "Do you have to be with me?" she asked him.

Ransom arched a brow. "What do you mean?"

"Do you have a choice, or are you forced to guard me?"

The corners of his eyes crinkled with laughter. "We chose each other. And I've got to say, you wanted me *bad*."

She playfully swatted his arm. "Seriously, I don't remember choosing you. When would I have done this?"

"Before you were born, when you knew what you were doing. I told you Clare, I know everything about you. More than you remember."

"Do you stay with me my entire life?"

He spread his hands. "I'm all yours. And as an added bonus, I help guide you toward the goals that your soul and I talked about."

An agenda before birth was foreign to Clare. And frankly, she found believing it a stretch. "What goals?" she asked.

"You have several, but your strongest desire is to fully know yourself as love and demonstrate what you know. It's an ambitious task," he admitted, and she saw admiration in his eyes. "That's why many are helping you."

Her head tilted. "Who's helping me?"

"Specifically?

She nodded.

"Well, besides me, you've got angels and saints, the ascended masters and loved ones, and your higher self, of course. Anyone you call on for help is with you in the same instant."

"Anyone?"

"Yes. But then be receptive to the messages. You've shut yourself off to much of your help these days."

This was news to Clare. "How have I shut myself off?"

"By choice. You choose everything. However, your soul remembers what it wishes to experience and pushes forward regardless. You're smart enough to know which way you're gently guided. Choose as the heart directs with confidence, and know you're supported in every heart endeavor."

She put a hand up. "Wait a minute. How do I get messages?"

"Guardians can talk to you directly through your mind, but often people aren't open to receiving help this way. Instead, we might cause you to notice a specific song on the radio with special meaning for you. Or we'll trigger a person to come into your life at precisely the right time with the exact information you need."

Clare frowned. "That's just coincidence."

"To you, this is how it seems. I assure you these happy, so-called coincidences are your helpers. Guardians can arrange clouds in different shapes, catch your eye with meaningful numbers, or call on nature for help."

"Like my butterfly?" she asked.

"Yes, like your butterfly. We also use feathers and coins. We drop them in special places where we know you'll find them."

Clare's jaw dropped. "I find pennies everywhere. I have jars filled with them."

Ransom grinned at her. "That's me letting you know I'm around."

"How come I haven't seen you before?"

"Your depressed vital energy put you at risk. It was my choice to take a physical form in order to help you."

"But why? Why do you want to help me?"

"I'm a guardian. My strongest desire is to protect and guide. It's what I do."

"That simple, huh?"

He shrugged. "Guardians don't go against our natures. It would be foolish, similar to jumping out of a plane without a parachute. Through our connection in Source, we are fully aware of every choice and what it creates. We make our decisions based on this knowledge."

"Nice for you," she said, unable to hide the frustrated envy in her tone.

Ransom gave her a curious look. "You think I have anything you don't? You're free to make decisions in the same way, with full awareness of what you create."

"Yeah, but this seems easier for you to do than it is for me," she whined. "How come?"

"My vibration is higher than yours."

"Aha!" She poked his chest with a finger. "You admit it's easier for you."

"Aha, nothing. My vibration is higher because I listen

to one voice. Something I'm encouraging you to do. That's why it's important to raise your vibration by watching the sunrise as we're doing. This is the time to recall your blessings with appreciation. Remember, gratitude brings more of what you appreciate."

Clare said, "You also told me gratitude combined with intention were unstoppable. What did you mean?"

"Giving thanks *before* you see your desire at the physical level is a declaration you know what you ask for is in the unmanifested state. Intention is calling your desire front and center from the live nothingness."

"Because whatever I focus on is real for me?" she asked.

"Yes. Subtle energy vibrations continuously stream from you, moving throughout the universe and beyond. Time means nothing. In the highest energy flow, your intentions create form instantly."

Clare shook her head, trying to get clear. If what Ransom said was true, the implications were huge. "Are you saying I can have whatever I desire?"

Ransom nodded. "It doesn't make any difference if it's a new job, a new relationship, or a bunch of loaves and fishes. At the highest levels you understand whatever shows up is perfect, and you've no need for life to be otherwise. This is the way masters live. They know on some level they are the creator of what they see or it wouldn't be there. They choose whatever life brings with love and gratitude. Do you remember why?"

Clare smiled. This answer she knew. "What we resist will persist. The way to change anything is to own the creation, love it, drop it, and choose again."

"That's my girl." Ransom broke into a grin, looking pleased. Clare couldn't help sitting a little taller. "Send your highest thoughts to the universe," he said, "and drop everything else. Physical life is a great tool when used as intended. When you forget who you are or what you're doing, even for a second, life can seem a hellish nightmare. You're the one who has to determine the side of life you believe is before you. Choose your thoughts with love for yourself and others, and you'll reap the benefits far into your future."

What Ransom was saying was interesting, but Clare found it created more questions. "You've taught me how to fill my chakra centers with sun energy, but are there other ways to raise my vibration?"

"As many ways as there are people," Ransom affirmed. "Sit quietly with your eyes closed and listen to the surroundings. Slowly turn your attention within and focus on your breath. Feel your heart beating inside your chest. Keep your focus within, and as the mind quiets feel your vibration rise. Stay with the sensation as long as possible."

"What else can I do to raise vibration?" she asked.

"You can stare at a flower, or a flame, or your hand, if you want to, as long as you don't get distracted by labeling. Trust you don't know what you're looking at as you turn within and feel the vibration rising. Quiet the mind and let Source show you what you see. I promise it will be a lot different and more accurate than what your brain tells you."

"My brother likes to run. He says it's spiritual for him."

"Run, jog, walk, lift weights, practice yoga, martial

arts, or exercise in whatever way you enjoy. To elevate vibration while exercising, concentrate on movement detail such as the breath filling the lungs, the muscles and tendons flexing and contracting, the elevated heart rate, perspiration on the skin. Feel every movement, and channel your thoughts toward appreciation for the movement. Gratitude lifts and aligns with the vibration of abundance."

"What if I can't take time to deep breathe or do any of the other stuff? What if I'm too busy?" Clare asked.

"Elevate your vibration by paying close attention to what you're *being* no matter what you're doing. Washing dishes, cleaning the house, eating, bathing. Are you appreciative for the ability to do these tasks, or has your mind carried you away? Take nothing for granted. Raise your awareness consciously by staying present and focused, and your vibration naturally rises."

The horses made restless noises inside the barn. It was breakfast time. Ransom stood and stretched, snatched the blanket from the hay, and pulled Clare to her feet. Watching the sunrise next to him had been cozy and warm, and provided a sense of well-being she hadn't felt in a long time. Away from his closeness, a chill ran through her.

"Cold?" Ransom asked. Concern on his face.

She nodded, and he wrapped the blanket around her shoulders. Clare gripped it tighter. "I was fine a minute ago."

"It's the high vibrations. You absorbed a megadose."

"Does energy change something in you?"

"Everything changes because your experience of what

130

is real for you changes, and experience is undeniable."

Ransom held his hands over Clare's head without touching her. Heart racing, a warm tingle washed over her body moving downward and out her feet. It was the biggest rush of her life. Nothing compared. Not even sex. Boy could she get used to this feeling.

Ransom smirked. Was he reading her thoughts? He'd better not be. "I want you to do something, Clare."

"What?" she managed to ask, though she had no idea how.

"Every morning when you wake, do deep breathing and stretching exercises to raise your vibration. Set your intention by saying: Today I listen with my whole heart, my whole mind, my whole being. Make this one simple change and your world changes. Can you do this? Can you make this a habit?"

Clare swallowed hard. "Will I feel like this?"

Again, the smirk. "You don't know the rapture that waits with the tiniest shift in your perception."

The barn door opened and Shannon Parker stepped out, pitchfork in hand. She clutched her chest with a gasp. "Oh! I didn't know anyone was back here."

Ransom said, "Not for long. We're heading inside."

Shannon followed them into the barn with a large forkful of hay and dropped it into Tuck's feed rack. The horse tossed his head and nickered his gratitude.

Clare watched the horse eat. "He looks happy."

"Thanks to the both of you," Shannon said. "The vet is coming out this morning to re-x-ray Tuck's knee, but I expect he'll be in for a big surprise." She gave Ransom a coy smile. "And thanks for last night. I owe you."

Clare furrowed her brow, and Shannon explained.

"I didn't want to leave Tuck alone, but I wanted the night with my husband, too. He's a lineman, and because of last week's ice storm he's been putting in crazy overtime. He got home around midnight and leaves again in a few hours. I won't see him for a week."

"Ah," said Clare with a knowing smile. "And Ransom stayed with Tuck for you."

"Insisted on it," she said. "I can't tell you how much I appreciate what you've both done. Your rooms are free, of course, but I'd also like to offer you a complimentary healing session with the horses."

Clare was bewildered. "How can horses heal?"

"They have a sensitive nature and accurately mirror our emotional state, helping us balance this energy. I can't explain how they do this, only that I've seen some incredible things."

Ransom looked excited. "Sounds great. When can we get started?"

Shannon hung the pitchfork in its place on the wall. "I'm finished with chores. How about now?"

Clare's hands got clammy. Horses made her nervous, they were too big. "Sorry. Count me out," she told Shannon. "There's no way I'm riding a horse."

"You won't have to," Shannon assured. "You're on the ground the entire time."

This news made Clare feel slightly better. She looked to Ransom for direction, and caught his nod. Obviously he thought the session was a good idea. If she were being honest, everything she'd done with Ransom made her feel braver and better about herself.

"I'm sick of my life," she confessed to Shannon. "If this helps me make positive changes, I need to do it."

Ransom gave her the thumbs up sign. It sort of felt good to have him proud of her.

"Okay, Shannon, we're in your hands," he said. "What do we have to do?"

A clipboard with a notebook hung on Tuck's door. Shannon tore out a couple sheets of paper and gave them each one, along with a pen. She said, "Think of one thing you desire more than anything else. Write it or draw it on the paper."

Clare sat on a hay bale, her back to Ransom, and clicked her pen in and out as she stared at the blank page. What did she desire more than anything else? She drew a heart within a circle representing the merging of Source with her heart.

Feeling embarrassed about asking for such a tall order, she shyly peered through her lashes at Ransom. "What did you ask for?"

He showed her his paper and her breath caught. He had sketched the same heart within a circle.

Looking over the drawings, Shannon raised her brows. "Spooky. That's never happened before."

Ransom grinned at Clare, and for once she knew what he was thinking—not spooky, a *coincidence*.

With hands on hips, Shannon instructed them. "Each of the horses outside represents a particular archetype. Pay attention to the horses drawn to you. They can help release patterns keeping you from your deepest desires." She eyed them. "Any questions?"

Ransom and Clare shook their heads no.

"Okay, follow me." She led them out the back door into the corral.

Chapter Fifteen

THE horses were in the pasture next to the corral, eating from a round bale feeder. Several tossed their heads and whinnied at the sight of people in their yard, others looked on without much interest as they calmly chewed hay.

Shannon swung the corral gate wide open, and two horses headed their direction. Clare stuck close to Ransom, her eyes apprehensive as the horses entered the ring. "Look at me, Clare," Ransom said, drawing her attention. "This will be a good experience, okay?"

Her nod was uncertain, but her chin lifted and Ransom smiled.

Several other horses abandoned their breakfast and filed into the ring milling about, sniffing the ground.

Shannon had Ransom and Clare focus on their drawings. "Visualize your life with the accomplishment of your desire."

Ransom imagined Clare glowing with joy and confidence, and felt a strong connection between her heart and his. When the majority of the horses were inside the corral, Shannon instructed them to spread out and put their paper on the ground by their feet. The horses with messages would come to them.

With a hesitant glance at Ransom, Clare chose a spot a few feet from the fence and set her paper down. Walking in the opposite direction, Ransom did the same with his paper.

Within minutes, a handsome stallion led two other

horses toward Clare. As they approached, she tensed, hugging her shoulders. "Oh, no, they're coming. What do I do?"

"This is great, Clare." Shannon's voice was encouraging as she walked closer. "Let them come."

The horses circled within a couple feet of Clare and stood like statues. "What are they doing?" she asked Shannon.

Shannon pointed excitedly. "See how they formed a circle around you like your drawing?"

Clare pivoted. "Oh my gosh, they have!" Her eyes cut to Ransom. "Look what they've done!"

Ransom barely had a chance to notice. A huge friendly draft horse kept nudging his shoulder, and there was no getting away from him. He followed Ransom wherever he went.

Shannon laughed when she saw him wrestling the old horse. "Brady's a big pest with a big message."

"I figured that out," he said, trying to give Brady the slip. "What does he want?"

"Ask him," she said, pulling up the hood of her jacket against the wind. She turned her attention to Clare and her circle of horses. "The black stallion came to you first," she observed. "He's all about releasing judgment." She gestured to the other horses. "The small paint is gentle and comes with the message of patience. The white mare brings compassion."

"How does this help me?" Clare asked with a guarded eye on the trio.

"Horses are emotion detectors. They reflect what you're feeling. These horses are telling you to release judgment about who you think you are and what you think is possible. You do this through compassion and gentle patience for yourself."

Clare hung her head. "Easier said than done," she admitted.

"This is about focusing on your desire and letting anything unlike it fall from your mind. It means monitoring your thoughts and feelings and noticing whether they're helpful without judging them as good or bad."

Clare looked surprised. "That's what Ransom says."

"He's right. Judgment is a deadly habit. I've often thought if judgments were burning lumps of coal in our hands, we'd drop them in a hurry."

Blinking back tears, Clare blew her nose, looking miserable.

"It's a big job," said Shannon gently. "Don't beat yourself up if you don't do everything perfectly. Keep weeding from your mind those things not in line with your desire and replace them with what you want. Changing a habit takes patience and practice, but it does get easier."

A fourth horse plodded over and joined the group around Clare. "Abby," Shannon smiled. "The love horse."

Abby touched her forehead to the mare's, and together they formed a heart. Clare gasped. "Did you see that? A heart!"

"A compassionate heart loves without judgment," Shannon said. "You are to love yourself unconditionally. This is their message."

Reaching out a tentative hand, Clare stroked Abby's face. "I hope I can learn to do that."

Ransom walked over to the women with the old draft horse following. Resting his chin on Ransom's shoulder, the horse blew out a contented sigh. Both women laughed.

Ransom narrowed his eyes. "How do I get this bugger off me?"

Shannon's expression softened. "Brady works with forgiveness. Specifically those people who can't move on with their lives until they forgive themselves."

Ransom grimaced. He hadn't expected to be blindsided with his own fear by a horse. This was a learning experience for Clare, not him. Then again, this was exactly how universal law worked, impartial and without judgment. Every thought unlike that of the Creator had to be brought to light in order to heal the suffering within. Hadn't he been explaining this to Clare?

Clare. He was suddenly aware she was watching him, large eyes blinking in shocked denial. She shook her head. "But you know everything. There must be a mistake."

Pain seared Ransom's heart as he held her gaze. It took all his might not to turn away. "I'm sorry."

Clare's face fell, and Ransom felt her disappointment. He turned into the horse, his shoulders quaking as his energy collapsed. This would not serve Clare. Yet here he was, trembling and powerless like one of his charges. He was in need of forgiveness. Forgiveness he'd been denying himself.

From the corner of his eye he saw Clare take a step toward him, but Shannon reached out and stopped her. "Wait," he heard her say quietly. "Brady knows what to do."

As if on cue, the big animal moved in closer and

wrapped his neck around Ransom. Immediately, he felt the horse's energy and knew he was in God's healing presence. Hugging the horse to him, Ransom fisted the mane, his chest tightening as his mind reeled recalling that horrible day. He didn't look at the women when he spoke. "I failed someone I promised to protect. He was eighteen when he died."

Ransom felt the weight of the women's stares on him. When he looked at Clare, he saw her deep concern. Some mighty guardian he turned out to be.

"What happened?" Shannon gently asked him.

A cold sweat pricked the back of Ransom's neck as the painful memory shuddered through him, weakening his knees. Thank God for the horse he clung to, or he wouldn't be standing. "I couldn't make him hear me," he said.

"A tall order for anyone," Shannon admitted, taking in his youthful features. "Especially for someone so young."

Ransom knew the age his appearance implied. For him, youth was a convenience enabling him to travel the world in physical ease, as there was no touchy stomach or aching joints to contend with. He could eat anything and fall asleep anywhere at the drop of a hat. People would be shocked if they knew he was billions of years older than the earth.

The big draft horse kept nudging Ransom, as if prompting him to talk. Soon, the nudging turned into a shove, and Ransom blew out a breath in surrender. "The guy I was to protect had been bullied most of his life," he told the women. "First by his parents, who had received the same treatment from their parents, and then by schoolmates who ridiculed and excluded him. They pushed him around while others turned a blind eye."

Shannon nodded knowingly, and Ransom continued.

"Angry and hurt, a plan took hold as a way to strike back for his pain. Something he'd seen on television. A few days later, he walked into a shopping center during a busy Christmas season and opened fire with a semi-automatic gun, killing two people and injuring five others. A man from mall security shot him from behind."

Clare sucked in a breath, horror on her face, and he couldn't blame her. No matter how many lifetimes he might decide to return to this planet, the gruesome scene was permanently etched in his mind.

"One of the people killed was a grandmother," he said, his voice breaking. He closed his eyes and gave in to the dark memories. "She'd moved in with her widower son and ran his house for him, helping out with the kids so he could go to work and not worry. She was at the mall enjoying a rare day to herself."

"Oh, no," he heard Shannon say, her voice filled with pity.

"The other person killed was an engineer who spent much of his free time and money on ways to improve living conditions in Africa. He dug wells and set up irrigation systems. An inventive mind, he was working on a gravity-powered generator as a cheap energy source to run their schools and hospitals." He looked at the women who were staring at him in grievous silence. "Can you imagine the miracle such a machine would've brought to poverty-stricken villages? It would've made survival a little easier for the poorest people on earth. Hopefully someone else will do this work, but there are no guarantees. One person unable to fulfill their destiny leaves a huge hole."

Ransom shook his head with regret, his chest heaving. "Of the five injured, several have recurring nightmares relieved somewhat by sleep aids and therapy. The security cop hadn't killed anyone before, and received a citizen's award for bravery from the city's police chief. A month after getting the award, he quit his job and relies on alcohol and antidepressants as a way to numb the memory. He's on the verge of losing his home and his marriage." Ransom gazed at the women. "If only…"

Clare walked to him, her lips quivering. Wrapping her arms around him, she hung on as if for dear life. A vibrational surge flowed through his body. Her heart energy expanded, encompassing him with compassion. The tingling warmth soothed his tortured heart, and the tightness in his chest eased.

Pulling back, she looked him in the eyes, her face wet with tears. "You're a great protector," she whispered hoarsely.

He squeezed her hand. There were no words to express what that meant to him.

Shannon came forward and stroked Brady's back. "Ransom, this wasn't your fault," she said softly. "While we don't always understand the choice of another, each of us is gifted with free will. It wouldn't be much of a life without it."

Ransom said nothing as he unearthed a small rock with his foot. Shannon meant well, but she was misguided. Choice implied an ability to make a selection affecting the greatest good. That was free will, and almost no one had this type of awareness.

"You disagree?" Shannon asked, watching him pick up the rock.

"Most people don't choose," Ransom told her. "They react. Most reactions stem from fear. In the grip of these dark emotions, a person is not free. Their mind is not their own, and their reactions are predictable. They must give what they have, and human suffering continues."

He flung the rock as hard as he could over the fence. The women looked to one another not knowing what to say.

Suddenly, Brady took hold of Ransom's hood with his mouth and tugged, dragging Ransom backwards around the corral. Tripping and flailing, Ransom twisted and pulled, trying to free himself. "What's he doing?" he called to Shannon.

The ranch owner looked mystified. "I don't know. It's the first I've seen him do this."

Alarmed, Clare took hold of Shannon's sleeve. "Can't you make him stop?"

"We don't want to do that," she said. "I believe the horses are divinely inspired to do what is necessary to facilitate healing. They stop when they sense a change in the person."

Ransom caught Clare's eye. She looked as bewildered as he by the horse's behavior, that is until her face lit with laughter. She trotted over to him and smiled good-naturedly. "Enjoying yourself?" she asked.

Enjoying himself? Had she gone mad? How could she think getting hauled around by a lunatic horse was enjoyable? And why was she laughing? Nothing about this was funny.

As he looked at her, an unfamiliar heat surged through him. An uncomfortable, irritating sensation churned in the pit of his stomach. His eyes narrowed. She should quit laughing before he did something to wipe the smugness from her face.

Walking alongside him, Clare lifted a brow. "Yikes. If looks could kill."

"What do you mean?" he asked.

"If I didn't know you were my guardian, I'd say you were on the verge of a meltdown."

A meltdown? Yes. That's how he felt, as if hot lava flowed inside him, cooking his brain. He couldn't think. He couldn't reason. He wanted to hit something—anything to rid himself of this horrible feeling.

Clare's eyes went wide. "Oh, my. You are having a meltdown." She grabbed the horse's halter. "Whoa."

Miraculously the horse stopped, but wouldn't let Ransom go. Coming around to face him, she forcefully grabbed Ransom by the shoulders. "Breathe," she said. "I'll do it with you."

Locking onto her eyes, he followed her lead, inhaling when she did and exhaling slowly. Within a couple breaths, the pulsing vibration lifted him to the familiar peace he was used to.

"Feeling better?" she asked.

He blew out another breath. "Much. Thanks."

"Listen to me, Ransom. Brady is the forgiveness horse. What if he's trying to show you how you've been dragging your feet, unwilling to forgive yourself? He's pulling you backwards to tell you to let go of the past and any mistake you think you made. We must say yes to what *is* because what we resist, persists."

His mind whirled. These were his words. This was the advice he'd given her.

She stood before him, eyes searching his. "If we can't change what is, we must willingly accept it and own it as our creation."

"Love the creation," he added softly.

"And drop it in order to create something new." She put her forehead against his. "Let's ask for help. Guardians protect you too, right?"

The question startled him. Of course he had protectors. How could he have forgotten? "No one is alone," he said.

"Good. More help." Squeezing her eyes shut, Clare recited her prayer. "Everything we need we have, even when we can't remember this is true. Thank you God for taking care of what we do not know. Let love, light, and healing energy flow through us for our highest good."

Waves of high energy rolled through Ransom, lightening his shoulders and quieting his mind. Gratitude swelled, filling his heart to near bursting, evaporating the heaviness he'd carried for so long. When was the last time he'd felt this free? In the same instant, the old horse dropped Ransom's hood and calmly walked away.

Lifting Clare off her feet, he squeezed her to him in a giant bear hug. "I feel great! Beyond great. Ecstatic! Thank you, God! And thank you, Clare Davis!"

Swinging her in a circle, she squealed with delight, eyes bright, cheeks rosy. His energy soared.

"You're a maniac," she giggled.

"I love being a maniac!" He set her on the ground. "Can you feel this energy? I mean, *wow*."

Clare's eyes dulled and her shoulders drooped. Her

smile slowly disappeared as she deflated in front of him, and he knew why. "You can't feel the energy, can you?"

She looked away from him. "I feel it...sometimes."

Taking her hand in his, Ransom tipped her face toward him. She looked like she wanted to cry. "Tell me what you're feeling."

"Seeing you so happy makes me want what you have, but I don't see how that's possible. I go to bed and hope the next day is better. It *has* to be better. I don't want to feel like this anymore. Morning comes and I wake in a cold sweat, gasping to catch my breath. Everything aches." She let out a long sigh, desperation in her eyes. "Nothing changes. I'm stuck. I can't move past whatever this is. I must be crazy."

"You're not crazy."

"Then what am I missing?"

Letting his mind go blank, an answer came to him. He took hold of her arm. "Come on. There's someone I want you to meet."

Chapter Sixteen

RANSOM and Clare said good-bye to the Parkers, and a couple hours later drove into Grand Marais. Built along Lake Superior at the base of the Sawtooth Mountains, the quaint harbor town was a mecca for artists and nature enthusiasts. It was also near the home of Dorothy Olson, a powerful healer Ransom was convinced could help Clare.

Ransom noticed Clare had a wistful look about her as they drove by a number of charming small shops. "What are you thinking about?" he asked her.

She blushed and gave him a sheepish sideways glance. "This town reminds me how much I'd love to have my own business designing women's clothing."

"Sounds fascinating. Care to share your plans?"

"Right. Like you want to talk about women's clothes."

"I do want to. It's important to be happy in your work. It's a big part of your life experience."

Her lips pursed, and he could tell she was deciding whether she believed him. Her tone was guarded when she spoke. "I've been thinking about creating a funky vintage line. One design would be a long, center-split skirt over a 50's-style swimsuit."

Ransom nodded. "I can see that."

With his approval, she relaxed enough to share more of her thoughts. "I want my designs personalized with a cool tag about the type of woman who'd wear the clothing."

"Such as...?"

"Well, the woman on the tag could be a dog rescuer, or a wildlife photographer, or a mother as comfortable in bright red lipstick as she is with spaghetti in her hair. Depending on the clothing sold, a percentage of the profits would go toward a correlating charity."

One look at Clare's excited face told him this was her heart's desire. "You should do this," he said.

She tilted her head. "Yeah? Didn't you say I was a healer?"

"Any person living as their heart directs *is* a powerful healer regardless of what they're doing."

Worry creased her forehead. "Except I don't have money to start a business. And if by some miracle I did manage to get a business going, how would I attract customers?"

The signal light turned red ahead of them, but Clare was oblivious, lost in her thoughts. "Red light," Ransom warned, hoping she'd slow the car.

"How would I pay my bills?" she asked herself, foot on the gas.

Ransom braced for impact. "Clare! Red light!"

Clare blinked wide, comprehension dawning. The tires screeched as she stomped on the brakes. Careening on the icy road, the car came to an abrupt stop halfway into the crosswalk with the seatbelts tight across their chests. Fortunately, there weren't any pedestrians in the street.

"Holy cripes," Clare gasped, knuckles white clutching the steering wheel. She looked over at Ransom. "Are you okay?"

Heart racing, he nodded, and wiped sweaty palms

on his jeans. After millenniums in and out of human form, how was it possible he hadn't grown immune to the adrenaline spikes triggered by the perception of danger? Such a curiosity. He'd experienced numerous deaths. There was nothing to fear.

He looked at Clare with her forehead against the steering wheel attempting to control her breathing. Compassion filled him. He put a hand on her shoulder. "No one's hurt. Everything's okay."

She gave him a shaky nod, her face pale. When the light turned green, she carefully checked both ways, squared her shoulders, and drove forward.

Ransom grinned. He didn't mean to, but there was something so darn admirable about her. It was her spunk, he decided. It was hard to be human.

She narrowed her eyes at him. "Don't you be smirking at me, Ransom Mayes."

He pretended to wipe the smile off his face.

"I'm serious. I didn't even see that light. How could I be looking at something and not see it?"

"Easy. You were in your mind and not present."

Groaning, she slapped her palm against her forehead. "I was. I was thinking about my business."

"More precisely, you were forming reasons why you couldn't start a business. What the mind believes, you'll see no matter the truth."

She blew out some air. "Am I ever going to get the hang of this? I mean, here I am getting tutored by my own private guardian. You'd think I'd be dancing on clouds, seeing auras all over the place."

Ransom laughed. "Let's keep this simple. Know what you desire and think of nothing else. You'll know what you desire by how you feel about it. Does the choice feel like something you *should* do, or something you *get* to do? Make the choice that feels like yippee—I get to do this! Don't choose anything that feels like an obligation. This is the way out of suffering."

"Does this concept apply to every choice?"

"Yes."

"What if I desire a romantic relationship with a person, but they're committed to someone else?"

"Like the last fellow you were dating?"

"You said to make choices based on what we want."

"I said the way out of suffering is to make choices that feel like *yippee*. This choice is from the heart and brings peace to everyone. If a single person suffers by your choice, the decision was made by the tiny speck of mind that created the world you see. That piece of mind has no peace."

"Never?"

"Never."

Annoyed, she rubbed her neck. "I'm trying to make better choices. What's it going to take for a lasting change?"

Ransom shook his head. "You're not looking for change."

"I'm not?"

"The entire physical universe is nothing but change. What you desire is a quiet mind. This allows recognition of the vast Creative Source flowing *within* you. There's no way to turn it off because *you are it*. Think of it, 100 percent power that automatically responds to your thoughts and emotions by moving living nothingness into form."

"Oh, dear God." There was fear in her voice.

"There's nothing to fear. When you're consistently aware of this power, everything changes *for* you. You *see* what you're creating. And with this tiny shift in perception comes an undisturbed peace. The world is as it is, but for you suffering is over because you no longer let the fearful mind control what you create."

Clare groaned. "It feels like my brain is in overdrive, thinking more crap than ever before."

"You're not thinking more, you're noticing *what* you're thinking more often. Congratulations. You're doing great."

Her eyes went wide. "How can you say that? Obviously I have way more thoughts than I catch, and you told me that's how we create our reality. Do you know how frightening that is?" She stared at him for a long second before turning back to the road. "No, I don't suppose you do, being who you are."

Ransom had to acknowledge she was right. By Divine design he remembered his origin, so he had no fear, and thank God for it. He'd be of no use to her otherwise.

Clare let off on the gas and sucked in some air. Ransom followed her pained gaze to a man holding open a door to a café at the end of the block. His resemblance to Clare's ex-fiancé was uncanny. Ransom looked twice to make sure it wasn't him. A woman stepped out of the restaurant and smiled at the man. The two strolled off hand-in-hand.

Ransom turned toward Clare. "Isn't today the anniversary of your engagement?"

She shook her head, tears welling. "Don't," she said. "I don't want to talk about it."

"Understood." He dropped the subject. Of course, he knew they'd soon be talking about her ex-fiancé in great detail, so no need to tick her off now.

They drove by the café and his stomach growled. "Let's eat."

Her expression turned suspicious. "I thought you were in a hurry to get to the healer."

"I am. Except I don't know where she lives, and I'm hungry."

"You don't know where she lives?" Clare was incredulous.

"Pull in here," he said, pointing to an empty parking space. "Someone in the café will know her."

Ignoring her long-suffering sigh, he was out of the car before she was parked. His mouth watered with thoughts of crisp bacon and eggs over easy, and he gestured for Clare to hurry her pace. When he opened the café door, the smell of espresso and freshly baked cinnamon rolls wiped the frown from her face. He struck up a conversation with the friendly hostess who escorted them to a corner booth. They learned the healer lived in the woods ten miles outside of town.

They ordered their food, and while they waited Clare's cellphone rang. Squinting at the number, her face registered surprise. "It's Shannon Parker."

Ransom had an uneasy feeling and moved closer to Clare in order to hear the conversation. Shannon sounded upset. "Two men driving a black SUV stopped by," she told them. "Big, scary brutes. The horses got agitated the second they stepped into the barn."

Ransom's hands fisted. He needed more time. She wasn't near ready to face them.

Clare's troubled eyes met Ransom's. She asked Shannon, "What did they want?"

"They wanted to know where you are. But don't worry, I didn't tell them. And besides, they won't be on your trail anytime soon." There was a hint of laughter in her tone.

"What do you mean?" Clare asked.

"Tuck managed to get out of his stall and into a bag of sweet feed. His stomach was rumbling and I was worried he'd end up with the trots. Sure enough, as I walked him, he let loose splattering everything in sight. Wasn't my fault those guys were standing too close. You should've seen their faces. Totally priceless," Shannon chuckled. "I gave them directions to the nearest laundromat."

Ransom couldn't help smiling. Good old Tuck.

"Anyway," said Shannon. "I wanted to warn you. Don't know what those yahoos want, but can't imagine it's anything good."

Chapter Seventeen

EVER since Shannon's phone call, a lump had lodged itself into the pit of Clare's stomach. She had wanted to go to the police, but Ransom was adamant they first see the healer.

They quickly left the restaurant, driving inland through the deep woods of the Superior National Forest—a remote wilderness dotted with dozens of lakes and winding rivers. If she hadn't been so scared of being followed, Clare would've enjoyed the view. A glance in the rearview mirror assured her there was nothing behind them except a white cloud of snow stirred by the car's tires.

"They are coming," Ransom said, his voice eerily resigned as he stared at the road ahead.

He'd never told her anything different, but she hadn't fully believed him. "Why?" she asked. "I've got nothing. No money, no boyfriend. No famous relatives I'm aware of. Why would anyone be after me? It's absurd."

A chilling thought struck her, one that pricked her scalp. She glanced over at Ransom, hands calmly folded in his lap. "It's you they're after, isn't it? You're the one with the high energy."

"My energy is high," he admitted, "But the vibration is beyond their immediate reality. To them I don't exist, other than as an occasional heart flutter." He turned toward her, and she read pain in his eyes. "You are the target, Clare, and you're drawing them to you."

"How? What am I doing?"

"It's not what you're doing," he said. "They're tracking you through what you're *being*. Remember how you found the injured horse in the barn?"

Clare thought back. She had known which stall the horse was in. How? And then it hit her. "They feel me," she said.

"Do you know why?" he asked.

She did know, and the realization made her stomach queasy. "Emotions are energy. I'm being fearful of nearly everything, and these people can feel my fear."

He nodded. "Whatever you're experiencing, whether high emotions or low, others subconsciously read the energy as if it was tattooed across your forehead."

Clare knew this was true. She'd known what her co-worker was feeling without him having said a word.

"But there's more to it than that," Ransom said. "When you're depressed, it seems like everything horrible that can go wrong does."

"Why is that?"

"Have you heard the expression 'like energy attracts the same'?"

"Yes. What does it mean?"

"Good or bad are one in the same. The Force within creates with impartiality."

Clare groaned. "And since I'm being fearful, I'll get that experience. I'm building a world on the outside to support the fear I have on the inside."

"Yes. And how do you change what no longer serves you?"

Clare knew this answer. "Step one is to own the creation as mine. Whether I remember or not, at some point I made what I see in my life. This knowledge helps

153

me love what I see as validation of the creative force working through me."

Ransom smiled. "Correct. How do you love the creation?"

Clare thought a moment. "By not judging it?"

Ransom gestured for her to go on.

"I turn within, surround myself in sparkling light, and notice the pulsing force inside me. This makes it easier to see the creation, whatever it is, as a gift without attaching labels such as good or bad."

"And what's wrong with judging something?" he asked.

"Truthfully? I don't know. Why shouldn't I decide if something is good or bad?"

"Labels of any kind keep you from seeing a bigger picture," he said.

"What do you mean?"

Ransom rubbed his chin thoughtfully. "Consider this: four aliens arrive on Earth, and each lands on a different part of the planet. One lands in the ocean, another on a mountaintop, another in the desert, and the last in the rainforest. Back home they compare notes, each believing they know what Earth is like. And based on their separate experiences, each view is correct, but nowhere near accurate when considering the bigger picture."

Clare's eyes lit. "You're saying my judgments are based on my perceptions created by my experiences, and when considered from a wider perspective are fairly limiting, especially since the Universe is limitless."

"Excellent," said Ransom. "Own whatever is in your life whether you remember creating it or not, otherwise you won't be aware of your creative powers."

Wow. The advice he gave her was huge! Essentially, she was stuck blaming others, unconsciously recreating the same scenario. She said, "It's within my power to change what I experience by accepting what *is* without judging or labeling. Look for the gift I sent myself, and with gratitude notice how the circumstance has best served me."

Ransom broke into a grin. "I couldn't have said it better. After loving the creation, what's next?"

"Withdraw my attention from it like a child drops a well-loved toy. This frees energy space and allows something new to appear in my life, something more in line with a grander version of who I am now."

Clare pressed her lips together. That was the plan, a grander version. Except she didn't have one. No matter what Ransom said, she knew the truth. She was nothing more than a weak, scared woman who messed up her career, her relationship, and her future. No wonder no one loved her, and she couldn't blame them. She was a disaster.

Ransom interrupted her depressed reverie. "Whose voice are you listening to?"

She could feel those clear, green eyes boring into her thoughts, and she gripped the steering wheel harder. "Get out of my head, Ransom. Guardian or not, I'm entitled to my privacy."

"Ha!" he snorted. "The *loud one* gives no privacy. The voice dominates your mind subjecting you to an unending loop of lies about who you are. It doesn't know the true source of your power. Unless you end the negative stream of thought, each insane fabrication becomes more distorted and hideous than the last.

"Trust your feelings. If they're not peaceful, use your safe word to break the thought stream. Take a deep breath and *choose* what you are *being*."

Clare blinked. Oh my gosh, what was she doing? Ransom was right. So quickly she'd gone from feeling strong and empowered, to a mind consumed by fearful regret. How had she slipped away again?

Glancing at Ransom, she noticed he was busy scrolling through pictures on a phone—*her phone. From her purse!* She grabbed for it, and he held it outside her reach.

He turned the phone so she could see. "Who's this next to you?"

The image was of a handsome man wearing glasses, his arm around her shoulders. Her heart skipped a painful beat as recognition cut her to the quick. *Adam.*

Ransom snapped his fingers as if something suddenly occurred to him. "It's your ex-fiancé. I knew I recognized the face. Remind me. Why did you dump him? You two made a nice couple."

Clare's temper flared. God, he was annoying. She snatched the phone from him and pocketed it. "Keep your hands out of my purse."

Ransom's eyes sparkled with laughter. "Look at you, Ms. Cranky Pants. You forget I know everything about you."

"Then you know the story. No need for me to elaborate."

"I counted forty-eight pictures of him, Clare, and I bet there's one in your wallet."

She was going to deny this, but closed her mouth. Their engagement picture was tucked behind her credit cards. Not that she looked at it…much. Exasperated, she narrowed her eyes at him. "Why are you bugging me about this?"

"He wanted kids and you didn't," he said.

"Yes, and you told me to accept what I can't change."

"Have you? Or is there a tiny part of you holding out for him to change?"

"You don't understand," she said. "The thought of having children makes me want to buy a one-way ticket to the Golden Gate Bridge. That might be a horrible thing to say, but it's the truth. I can't be a mother. It'd be a huge mistake. I *know* it."

"Why do you think that?" His tone was gentle.

She was at a loss. How many times had she asked herself this same question? There wasn't a reason for her to feel as she did. Nothing she could think of anyway. It was infuriating. Pressing on the gas, Clare aimed her frustration at Ransom. "Not everyone's cut out for children."

"True. Not everyone is," he agreed.

"Adam should love me no matter what, even if I don't want children." She lifted her chin, feeling justified.

Ransom nodded wholeheartedly. "And you also love yourself no matter what, I assume?"

"What?"

"You love yourself unequivocally, with or without Adam, or children, or a job, or money, or anything outside yourself. That's why you're so happy. Because you love yourself so much."

Clare's breath caught and the road blurred in front of her. How could he throw such a horrible thing in her face? He knew she tried to end her life. In fact, he took every opportunity to point out how well he knew her.

A bitter taste filled her mouth. She glanced his way. "Are you trying to be cruel?"

"No." His expression was sincere.

"How can I be happy? The man I love wants children more than he wants me."

"Clare," Ransom said softly. "You don't need his unconditional love for you to love yourself unconditionally."

She sniffed. "Relationships are nothing but trouble anyway."

"Seems true, doesn't it? Especially if you think a relationship will make you happy."

She bristled. "Shouldn't it? Why be in a relationship if you're not happy?"

Ransom folded a stick of gum into his mouth. Clare had no doubt the gum came from her purse. He said, "Hate to burst your bubble, but happiness has nothing to do with it. Relationships create opportunity for experiencing your authentic nature."

"Authentic nature? You mean love?" she asked.

"You are the natural expression of love revealed in physical form. When you see as God does, you won't need anyone to be anything other than who they are.

"This is the function of *every* relationship, whether it's romantic, friendship, with a co-worker, a family member, a pet, or a plant. Relationship is the communion with Creator and created."

Clare stared at the road in front of her. "So what is love? I mean real love, like the God love you're talking about?"

"Bliss."

Ransom relaxed against the seat, his beautiful eyes lit by the thought. Clare felt a stab of envy. She wanted what she saw in Ransom's face. He said, "True being is that which has no conditions, requests, motives, rules, expectations, boundaries, limits, or ties of any kind."

He turned those crystalline eyes her way and it was as if the sun was shining on her from the inside out. In that moment she felt invincible. He said, "When you're told that love conquers all, you think it wonderful. But to conquer, one must be in conflict with another. Love is not conflicted and sees itself reflecting perfectly in every form, including you.

"You are Life's Orgasmic Vital Energy. You are LOVE, timeless and formless. You have no conditions, expectations, or rules to obey to be who you are. You merely need demonstrate what you know, creating the experience. Without experience, love is a belief at best."

Clare chewed her lip. "What stops me from noticing I'm LOVE?"

"Your fear."

"What fear?"

"The fear-based insanity living inside your head, and the heads of most people. It incessantly worries, judges, excludes, regrets, wants, defends, and a whole slew of other craziness. It rarely, if ever, applauds your efforts, or anyone else's. If every thought was said aloud, everyone would quickly recognize the dysfunction for what it is."

Clare was more depressed. She'd been backing the wrong horse. "How do relationships wake us to our true nature?" she asked.

"They precisely reveal the quality of your thoughts and emotions."

"How?"

"Do you remember how upset you were in the store yesterday when you threw the sign and hit your boss?"

Clare inwardly cringed. She hadn't thought of Joanna for what seemed an eternity and was in no hurry to think of her now.

Ransom leaned toward her. "Do you remember what you felt?"

Did she ever! She boiled just thinking about the things Ransom had said to her boss. Private things he had no right to say. He had made a fool out of her in front of everyone.

"Talk to me, Clare," he said, looking at her. "How did you feel?"

She stiffened, meeting his eyes briefly. "You embarrassed me."

"And how did that feel?" he prodded.

"I wanted to kill you!" The words exploded from her. Who would blame her? No one, that's who! What he did was wrong. More than wrong. What Ransom did was inexcusable. He needed to get on his knees and beg her forgiveness. Knowing him, he probably figured she owed him an apology, like everything was her fault. He didn't care about her. He was just like Adam and Keith and every guy she ever dated. Well, fat chance, buddy. You're not getting anything from me!

Ransom drew back from her. "I'd say a penny for your thoughts, but I'm sure I don't want them. From the way it looks, you're on a roll."

Clare froze, and a chill went through her. Oh, God,

her thoughts. And worse! She had told her guardian she wanted to kill him. How had this happened? They were talking, and then... And then she lost her mind! No. She let her mind wander and was living in the past listening to the *loud one*.

Gah! She slapped her forehead. *Butterfly, butterfly, butterfly!*

Ransom waved a hand in front of her face. "Hi there, nice to have you back. Do you see how relationships help wake you? It's nearly impossible to be objective about your own insanity, yet it's easy to recognize it in someone else. Of course, you'll believe it's *their* issue, or *their* problem, not yours."

Clare was mortified. "I didn't mean what I said."

"Yes, you did."

She was about to protest, but Ransom held up his hand. "If I hadn't said something, would you have wanted to quit what you were thinking?"

The answer stunned her. "No. It's like I was possessed. I didn't know what I was thinking."

"That's more accurate than you know. Left unchecked, your mind traps you for hours, days, sometimes months in its distorted reality, draining your energy and raising havoc with the body's immune system."

"Okay. Now I'm scared," Clare said.

"You don't have to be. Relationships are huge blessings no matter their appearance. Have you noticed the way people comment about quirks or habits in others that they also have and don't see? Like someone who complains about a co-worker who's always late, yet they act the same way."

Clare didn't have to think hard to come up with

people she knew who were like this.

"When you have the urge to condemn someone for whatever they're doing or saying, know this same trait is something *you* need to work on or it wouldn't have bothered you."

Ahead, the road dead-ended into a driveway criss-crossed with animal tracks. The name on the mailbox said OLSON. The box was a miniature version of a Victorian house, complete with gingerbread trim. Clare hadn't expected to see anything this dainty in the wilderness.

After she drove another quarter mile through dense woods, a clearing opened, exposing a large Victorian house identical to the mailbox. The two-and-a-half-story home was painted salmon pink with a wraparound porch dripping in cream-colored spindle work. Lace curtains hung in the candlelit windows.

The hairs on Clare's arms stood on end the second she saw the house. Overwhelmed with dread, she eased up on the gas. She had the unsettled feeling she was driving to her death.

Chapter Eighteen

SLOWLY, Clare drove to the front door and parked. The spot between her shoulder blades throbbed painfully, as if a knife had been thrust into her back. "Is it absolutely necessary I see *this* healer?" she asked Ransom.

His clear eyes pierced hers. For once, she hoped he was reading her thoughts. He'd know how much she wanted to drive away and never come back. Instead, he instructed her to close her eyes and breathe deeply. It wasn't long before pulsing energy filled her body with vibrating warmth.

"Keep breathing," Ransom said. "And ask yourself if this person can help you."

Before Clare had time to think, the word 'yes' popped into her head. The answer came to her quietly and without emotion, similar to intuition except with more certainty. Seeming to sense her answer, Ransom was out of the car before she could object.

Clare trailed him up the porch steps, feet dragging. Pine boughs and winterberries decorated window boxes and the tall urn by the etched glass door. Lovely touches, yet everything about the place made her skin crawl. Ransom rang the doorbell, and she had all she could do not to run away shrieking.

An older woman opened the door wearing linen slacks under a low-cut, lacy tunic that made the most of her ample bosom. She was attractive in the pampered way Clare couldn't afford to be with flawless makeup, manicured nails, and coiffed hair swept into an elegant knot. Dangling from her ears were ornate gold earrings unlike any Clare had seen, and the gemstone rings she wore would easily pay off Clare's loans with money left for a small house.

The woman peered briefly at Clare, and then her gaze fell on Ransom. With her hand on a curvy hip, her eyes traveled over the length of him. "Well, well, who do we have here?" she asked.

Ransom grinned like a lunatic at her flirtatious tone until Clare elbowed him. Straightening, he made their introductions. "We've come for a healing session," he told her. "Are you Dorothy Olson?"

"Dot," she smiled coyly, opening the door wider for them to enter. "No one calls me Dorothy except my *extremely* ex-husband."

She seductively played with her earring, obviously for Ransom's benefit. Clare rolled her eyes. The woman had to be at least sixty.

Fighting an increasing feeling of alarm, Clare followed Ransom inside to the foyer, stepping onto a thick Persian rug. She pulled off her hat smoothing her hair, her eyes adjusting to the dim light of a bronze chandelier embossed with tiny cherubs. Museum-quality paintings adorned rich paneling, and delicate porcelain angels filled a curved-glass cabinet. Clare would've loved a chance to study them, except she couldn't take her eyes from the sweeping staircase and the masterly carved newel post in the form of a male nude. Clearly this was a woman of refined taste, if not slightly odd.

Dot closed the door and hung their coats in a closet. Taking Ransom's arm, she ushered them into the front parlor. Clare stopped dead in the archway with the crazy thought she'd been in this room before. Impossible, she knew. The room was straight out of Victorian 19th century—antique furniture, heavy draperies, starched doilies on every surface. An oil painting of Adonis, the Greek god of desire, hung above the fireplace. This was nothing like the 70's ranch home of Clare's childhood, yet she knew she *belonged* in this space.

The feeling disturbed her, and she quickly took a seat on a dainty sofa next to Ransom. The cushions were rock hard, aggravating her back pain. "Your home is lovely," she told Dot, who had settled onto a small armchair across from them.

Dot smiled graciously. "Not the typical log cabin you'd expect in these wilds, but I'm not your typical old lady." Dabbing perfume behind her ears, she batted her lashes at Ransom. "What can I do for you, love?"

"Not me," said Ransom, clapping a hand on Clare's shoulder. "But Clare's here for the works. Whatever she needs."

Dot briefly eyed Clare before returning her attention to Ransom. Lightly tracing her cleavage with the tip of her finger, she bit on her lip and openly stared at him, desire burning with enough intensity to power the Northern Hemisphere. "Are you sure there's nothing I can do for you?" she asked.

To Clare's surprise, Ransom chuckled self-consciously, color rising in his cheeks. His eyes were brighter than she'd seen them before. Was the unflappable Ransom blushing?

Clare was used to the way women stared at Ransom. By every appearance, he was a good-looking young guy.

Coupled with his high energy vibration, who could blame anyone for being drawn to him? However, this woman was openly throwing herself at him and he was genuinely flattered, as if he were enjoying the attention.

Clare studied Dot. What was it about this woman? She was attractive, but not *that* attractive. Not like she would've been in her younger years. Yet Ransom was clearly enthralled, and obviously interested in what she had to offer. What was happening?

Shifting in his seat, Ransom pulled at his collar. "I'm sorry," he said to Dot, sounding deeply apologetic. "Today is for Clare."

Dot's eyes danced with amusement, and after a long moment sighed dramatically. "Of course. Pity, though." She looked like she truly meant it. Her attention shifted to Clare and she rose from the chair. "Give me a minute, dear. I'll get things ready for you."

Dot sashayed from the room in a whiff of jasmine, and Clare turned to Ransom. "Exactly what type of healing does she do?"

A sappy smile stretched across his face. "She's a past life regressionist. She helps people access previous lives that might be interfering with their current life."

Clare felt her mouth fall open. "You're talking about reincarnation."

He looked at her. "You seem surprised."

"I was taught we have one life. How am I supposed to believe this?"

"What did we say about beliefs?"

"Uh, that we're not supposed to have them?"

"Why?"

"Beliefs are part of a limited thought system. Source

166

is limitless."

"And if you want to experience the Source of All?"

"Don't rely on beliefs. God is a felt experience and can't be explained in words."

Ransom sat forward. "Try to keep an open mind, Clare, and remember, as of yet you do not see as God sees. If you did, there'd be nothing in your heart except total joy and gratitude for the gift of your life and everyone in it."

Since Clare couldn't say with any honesty she found her life a total joy, she agreed to at least listen to what Dot had to say. "By the way," Clare said, staring sideways at Ransom, "what was the flirting about? I wanted to turn a hose on you both."

 "Yeah, I know," he said, blowing out some air. "Tough to turn down Aphrodite."

Clare blinked at him. "Did I hear you right? Aphrodite? Greek goddess of love?"

Ransom's sappy grin returned. "Bet she gives a wonderful massage."

Ransom chose to wait in the parlor as Dot led a nervous Clare through a back hallway and into an opulent library. Ancient books lined the shelves, many in languages Clare didn't know existed. A sofa loomed at the room's center and she stared at it, a tight ball forming in her stomach. When Dot closed the door, Clare spun on her heels, her nerves kicking into high gear. "I'm sorry, I've changed my mind. I'm not ready for this."

"We won't do anything you don't want to do," Dot gently assured, every trace of vixen gone.

She gestured to the sofa, and Clare sat on her hands to keep them from shaking.

Dimming the lights, Dot closed the draperies. "Have you had a past life regression?"

"No," Clare admitted. "Ransom said something about a way to access a previous life? Then again, he thinks you're Aphrodite."

"Mmm," Dot purred. "Sweet boy."

Clare raised her brows. "Even if it's possible to have a regression, I'm not that comfortable with the idea. How can something be real if you can't remember it?"

"Do you remember being born?" Dot asked. "Yet here you are. A regression is a way to release memories that no longer serve the life you're experiencing, and it's accomplished through focused forgiveness."

"What's focused forgiveness?" Clare asked.

"A state where you're guided to witness the past as if you're watching a movie without judgment of anything you see or feel. You'll let thoughts and emotions move through you as you release the experience to Source."

"What if it doesn't work on me?"

"Everyone has the ability to access their past."

Clare hesitated, unsure what to do. Ransom brought her here for this experience, but the whole idea was so foreign to her.

Dot leaned toward her. "A journey into your past is intensely personal and different for everyone. Think of it as an opportunity to heal something that's hurting you."

"How will I know it's not my imagination?"

"Many of my clients' regressions are of common, everyday lives. I figure if they were going to invent a story, it'd at least be more exciting."

Clare considered this. "What if I get stuck in the past,

or do something I don't want to do?"

"You won't do anything you wouldn't do normally, and you can't get stuck. Even if I dropped over in the middle of your session, you'd merely wake and hopefully call 9-1-1," she joked. "What do you say, Clare? Would you like to try a session?"

Chapter Nineteen

CLARE'S resolve was weakening. Dot assured her she'd remain conscious during the regression and could end the session whenever she wanted to. Clare finally decided if this therapy could help her feel better about herself, why not try it? What did she have to lose?

Dot had Clare lie on the sofa and covered her with a soft blanket. Pulling up a chair, Dot began the session. "We ask the guides and angels to wrap Clare in protective healing light, and reveal whatever is of greatest benefit for her in this lifetime."

Clare was led through a series of relaxation techniques, and as the tension released, her body went limp. Dot said, "When you're ready, see yourself standing in a hallway with doors on either side."

To Clare's amazement, a long, narrow hallway with lots of doors appeared in her mind's eye. Drawn to a purple door with an ornate brass knob, she opened it and found herself in a vast field of straw-colored prairie grass stretching as far as the eye could see. A breeze stirred the grass into gentle waves and her heart soared with joy. "I'm standing in the middle of a prairie," she told Dot.

"Look at your feet. What kind of shoes are you wearing?"

Clare was shocked to see she was staring at the bare feet of a small child. "I'm about six years old and I'm not wearing shoes."

"What are you wearing?"

"A long dress and apron, like a pioneer."

"What color is your hair?"

"It's long and almost yellow."

"Do you have anything in your hands?" Dot asked.

"A wooden bucket filled with dirty white roots."

"Where do you live?"

A scene unfolded in Clare's mind as if she were watching a movie. She saw the girl, whom she positively knew to be herself, sitting inside a primitively constructed dwelling with mud walls and floor. Above her head was a ceiling of thick, bundled grass. The dim room was lit by a kerosene lamp. She said, "I'm in a cabin sitting at a long wooden table."

"Are you alone?" Dot asked.

"I'm with my family eating supper."

"What are you eating?"

"Brown gravy and bread. We're laughing. My brother told a joke."

"Are you happy?"

"Yes."

"Okay, let's leave this place and ask to see what you need to heal."

Immediately, Clare saw a plush 19th-century parlor with a beautiful curved glass window. A woman sat in front of a marble fireplace mechanically rocking a screaming infant. She wore a high lace collar and full-length skirt. Her face was pale and drawn as she blindly stared into the fire, oblivious to the wild clamor of a half-dozen young children playing in the room around her. The woman was the same little girl Clare had seen in the field. Her depressed thoughts filled Clare's mind, although there wasn't any emotion with them.

"Where are you?" Dot asked.

"I'm inside an expensive house with lots of children. They're making a ton of noise and I don't like it. I don't want to be here anymore."

"You don't want to be in the room?"

Clare shook her head, and the swiftness of the next thought startled her. "I'm going to jump off a bridge."

The thought had barely occurred to Clare before a dusky scene unfolded in front of her. The woman was standing at the edge of a high bridge gripping a cold steel cable as the wind whipped her cape about her. Below, the swift current churned the black water into a deathly cauldron. The woman closed her eyes to the terror one small step away. Blessed relief was her only thought before she let go of the cable.

Clare did not see her fall. What she saw was the woman's body face down, washed along the shoreline, her white knickers exposed under a wet skirt bunched to her knees. Gulls screeched as waves rolled in. A policeman walked the water's edge, eyes searching the ground. Several others stood guard over the body.

"They found her body," Clare said. "Her husband is standing a few feet from her and he's grief-stricken. There's a young boy about twelve at his side. His eyes are dark and he's mad at her."

"Do you know who they are in this life?" Dot asked.

Unexpectedly, Joanna came to mind. Clare looked again at the boy. His eyes were the same as her former boss's. There was no mistake. "I know the boy," she said.

The scene faded, and outlined in a golden glow the woman stood in front of Clare, her gentle eyes radiant. Clare felt nothing toward the woman except a mild sense of curiosity. "Why did you jump?" she asked her.

"My husband loved me and provided well, but I was terribly unhappy. Instead of following my inner guidance, I made safer, easier choices, and married a man I didn't love."

"What choice were you supposed to make?"

"I'm a healer. Many of my previous lives have been difficult because I spoke my truth. I was afraid to follow my heart in this life."

As soon as the woman finished speaking, Clare glimpsed an ancient time where she saw a man in white robes at the base of a mountain teaching a large group of people. When the teacher moved through the crowd, a man from behind buried a hatchet into the teacher's back. It was in the exact spot between the shoulder blades Clare felt when she was stressed. The teacher's protectors rushed in, walling him from the panicked crowd. The teacher turned to face his attacker and Clare gasped. The man's eyes held the same rage she'd seen in the boy's eyes. The implications were undeniable.

"I'm the teacher," Clare said to the woman, "but I'm also you as a young mother."

The woman nodded. "The man who murdered the teacher believed he was protecting people from a powerful liar who would destroy them."

"What happened after you jumped off the bridge and died?" Clare asked.

"No one dies. Life is ongoing."

"Okay, what happens after we drop our bodies and

end the human experience?"

"The 'human experience,' as you call this moment, does not end. The person drops the body, not the mind. They come to understand what they wished to create with the body and, based on their *own* evaluation of their earth life, decide whether to 'come back' into human form."

"Is the choice different for someone who ends their own life?" Clare asked.

"Suicide is a misunderstanding between the mind and the heart," the woman said. "When the person dies, they understand this well and reincarnate. It's not a painful procedure. It doesn't cause guilt or regret or any form of negativity for the soul. It's simply what happened and is viewed without painful emotion. At my death, I was embraced and fortified with loving light, and made the choice to finish my soul's agenda."

The woman looked kindly into Clare's eyes. Her fingertips grazed Clare's cheek and warmth spread through her.

"Child, you are loved," she told Clare. "You are meant to feel and make real every aspect of your true being. It's okay—perfectly okay to have done, and been, and felt, and chosen *everything* you have. It's what everyone is doing on the physical plane. It's your great blessing.

"If there is karma you undertake, let it pass willingly without a troubled heart. You cannot fully know how each of your moments, or those of others, fits into the greater whole. Move with the freedom of knowing whatever happened, whatever the reason, you did perfect for the small moment you call 'time'. Ultimately, you've done no harm, no wrong. You've nothing to fear, and neither does anyone else."

"How do I know my soul's agenda?" Clare asked.

"The Creator's great love is expressed through Divine Grace, which you feel as glorious inspiration. Whatever desire is in your heart is there as your great blessing. To act on your heart's wishes is to follow the gentle nudging of your soul. Let yourself enjoy the process of Life lived through you. This is total freedom. Freedom is *who you are.*"

The woman faded and Clare found herself standing in the hallway outside the purple door. Dot counted backwards from five to one, and Clare opened her eyes. She was back in the library, lying on the sofa beneath the blanket, with a smiling Dot sitting in a chair beside her. "Welcome back," she said.

Clare blinked at her. "At least I know why I thought I'd damage any children I had. Her death couldn't have been easy for her family. I know the boy felt betrayed."

Suddenly, it hit Clare how many times she'd felt betrayed by Joanna. A 'backstabber', she'd called her, and thought again of the pain she experienced regularly between her shoulder blades. Could this be the result of a hatchet in the back from a past life?

Throwing off the blanket, Clare sat and looked at Dot. "It's weird how the past affects our current lives."

"Honey, don't I know it," Dot sighed. Her rings caught the light as she poured water into a crystal goblet. She handed the heavy glass to Clare. "Can't look at a man without imagining what's in his pants, and I don't mean his wallet. Although lord knows, I do appreciate a well-endowed wallet."

Clare had to smile. She was warming to Dot. Sipping the water, she thought of another question. "How can our body remember something we can't?"

"Because your body is contained within your soul and your soul is the manifested essence of the Life Force. This Living Force remembers everything because it *is* everything."

"Wait. Are you saying our soul isn't inside our body?"

"Your body is in and surrounded by the soul. It's a bit like a fish in the ocean. The fish is in the water, surrounded by water, and from the water, yet uniquely separate." Dot edged forward in her chair. "But I warn you, as a soul who decided to incarnate for the purpose of exploring physicality, you must pay attention to your thoughts, words, and actions. This world is not yours alone, and what you create affects more than you know."

Clare nodded. "I'm starting to realize that. If I want to end an unpleasant cycle of hurt, I must see every circumstance as a gift of my own creation, and in this way I honor the powerful force within me. Then I can make a new choice, something more in line with my heart's desire."

"I couldn't have said it better," Dot beamed. "You can also cut cords and send light to heal anything, including your past."

"Cut cords?" Clare had never heard of such a thing.

"Energy cords," Dot explained. "Sometimes fear-filled invisible cords attach to you from other people, or objects, or from places. Since energy is not bound by time or space, it's important to cut any cords that might be draining you."

"How do I do that?"

Dot flicked her hand. "I ask the angels to do it. Archangel Michael uses his sword and cuts away anything I don't need, and Archangel Raphael fills the empty space with beautiful healing light."

"What if a person doesn't believe in angels?"

"Not a problem," Dot said. "Visualize a giant golden scissors cutting the cords and a sparkling caulk gun filling the space with radiant light. Either way works. I cut cords every morning when I wake and every night before I go to sleep. It's incredibly invigorating."

Taking a tube of lipstick from her pocket, Dot applied a fresh coat of red to her lips. "Speaking of invigorating. I hope that handsome man of yours hasn't gotten too lonely."

Clare didn't bother explaining that Ransom wasn't her man, because Dot was already racing from the room. Pathetic the way she chased after Ransom. There had to be forty years difference between them. She would never behave so ridiculously.

Retracing her steps through the hallway, the nagging thought occurred that she had been equally ridiculous, if not more so. Clare's stride slowed. Hadn't she been the one to run to the nightclub after Keith? A man she knew in her heart she couldn't trust? And the way people looked at her that night, judging her pathetic as she stood in the middle of the dance floor staring at him with that woman. For crying out loud, Dot probably had a better chance with Ransom than she'd had with Keith.

Guilt burned Clare's cheeks. Ransom was right. The

behaviors that bothered her in someone else were the same ones she needed to work on. Judging Dot, or any circumstance, would keep her stuck in the same downward cycle.

Clare found Dot in the parlor standing by a table with an answering machine flashing a message. In her hand was a single sheet of paper. She looked from the paper at Clare, her expression bewildered. "He's gone."

"What do you mean, he's gone?" Clare's heart beat faster as she peered out the window. No car. She snatched the note from Dot's hands. Before she could read it, Dot pressed the answering machine. A man's voice sounded urgent. He was from a neighboring lodge, and a guest of theirs, a pregnant woman, was in labor having difficulty. He was looking for the doctor.

Clare raised her eyes to Dot. "Doc Adams is a frequent visitor," she said. "People usually call here first."

Was there no male on the planet not charmed by this woman? Clare sucked in a breath. What was she doing? How easily she'd gone back to judging. At least she noticed this time. Hadn't Ransom told her that was the first step—to catch her thoughts as she had them?

Her mind turned to her guardian. People who wanted to harm her were looking for her. Why would he leave? To help the pregnant woman? Clare looked at the paper in her hand. In Ransom's messy scrawl she read:

Clare,

The baby in trouble is the young man who killed those people in the shopping mall. I'm not about to lose him again. Sit tight and practice raising your vibration.

P.S. Is it okay if I borrow your car? You can let me know when I get back.

Chapter Twenty

STARING at Ransom's note, Clare's vision blurred and dark spots danced on the paper. A sharp pain stabbed the left side of her head, making her wince. Great. A migraine. Just what she needed.

"Hon, are you feeling okay?" Dot asked. "You look green."

"Migraine," Clare said through gritted teeth.

Her stomach lurched and she headed for the door. No way was she getting sick in Dot's fancy house. The room started to spin, and Dot came to her aid, putting an arm around her waist. Stumbling out onto the porch, Clare grabbed the railing and eased herself onto the top step. Shivering, she hugged herself for warmth. Dot went back inside for Clare's coat.

Closing her eyes, Clare breathed in the frigid air. With each intake, she visualized Archangel Michael pulling the painful energy spikes from her brain. On her exhales, she pictured warm, golden light filling the space in the same way as Ransom had done for her in the car at the gas station.

By the time Dot returned with her coat, Clare's headache was nearly gone. A major surprise, since migraines often wiped her out for days.

Dot wrapped her shawl tighter about her, assessing Clare with an approving eye. "You're looking much better."

"I feel better." Clare got to her feet and buttoned her coat. "Do you mind if I walk around? The fresh air helps."

"You go ahead, hon. If you're up to it, there's a nice trail through the woods leading to a waterfall."

That sounded perfect to Clare.

Pointing, Dot directed her beyond the lawn to a gap in the trees. "Course you want to keep track of the time. It gets dark early in the woods. I'd go with you, except someone should be here when Ransom gets back."

Lowering her long lashes, Dot was the picture of piety. A real Mother Theresa, Clare thought, for men in need of a good lay. Oops. That might be judging.

Entering the woods, Clare followed a narrow path, her boots crunching the snow. Two fluffy squirrels chased around and around a soaring aspen not caring she was watching them play. There were tracks everywhere—deer, rabbits, turkeys. Hopefully the paw prints she saw belonged to a large dog. The thought of wolves in the woods had her on high alert. All of a sudden every shadow was a crouching beast ready to spring into action.

She stood for a moment, her heart racing, deciding whether to turn back, until she noticed the way the pale afternoon light streamed through the trees. The golden rays shimmered and pulsed, the intense beauty stirring something profound within her. Clare breathed deeply, feeling the vibrational current running through her body. She listened to the peaceful noises around her: birds chirping, the hollow knocking of a woodpecker, wind rustling the treetops. In the distance, she heard the sound of flowing water.

The waterfall. She wanted to see the waterfall.

With a renewed sense of excitement, Clare forged ahead, the falls getting louder with each step. Within a few minutes she was standing at the end of the trail, peering into a deep gorge. The river wasn't much more than a dark, twelve-foot wide slit snaking through layers of snow and ice. At the top of a rocky ledge, wide, jagged curtains of thick, milky ice hung on either side of a narrow falls. Misty spray shrouded boulders at the bottom in what looked like frozen mounds of foam.

Out in the open, a cold breeze whipped her hair and stung her face, yet Clare lingered, unable to tear herself from the stunning view. Without trying, her energy soared in the presence of such beauty, expanding her heart with an immense sense of gratitude that was borderline painful. Her whole body vibrated. She felt free, as if everything was possible and there wasn't anything she couldn't do. A vision came to mind, and she saw herself happy, excited, designing fashions for her own stores using organic, earth-friendly textiles.

Abruptly, she heard a twig snap and the sound of someone behind her. Heart in her throat, she whirled around and saw two men approaching from the woods. Built thick and powerful, the men were an intimidating sight dressed entirely in black. One was white haired and fair skinned; the other dark with a lumberjack's beard.

Eyes scanning their surroundings, they closed to within a few feet of her. The bearded man cracked his knuckles. "You're a hard woman to find," he said.

d

The sun was sinking behind the trees when Ransom turned onto the road leading to the regressionist's home. Rubbing his neck, he rolled his head from side to side easing the tension from his body. He was thankful for these few quiet moments alone to regroup before facing

Clare's wrath for taking her car again.

It had been touch and go with the child. He'd been resisting his birth, unwilling to leave the womb's security. Could be he was coming into the world with too much unresolved human fear in his memory.

Ransom heaved a tired sigh. If humans knew how much they were loved, their fear would dissolve instantly. It was their greatest blessing, yet meant nothing if they couldn't experience the gift.

How could he get them to understand? The stream of love was full and complete and ever-present without stipulations. And if that wasn't enough, millions of un-employed angels stood by waiting for someone to ask for a miracle. What were people waiting for?

While he mulled over this thought, he caught sight of a black SUV parked along the shoulder not far from Dot's driveway. The muscle in his jaw tightened. Easy, he told himself. Lots of black SUVs on the road. Could be a hiker.

Slowing to get a better look, he saw the rental barcode stickers on the windows and knew it was them. *They found her.*

Gripping the steering wheel tighter, Ransom stomped on the gas, racing up the winding drive, the Camry's backend swerving as the car skidded to a stop. Bolting from the car, he took the porch steps two at a time, his heart hammering. He burst through the front door. "Clare!"

No answer, only silence.

The hairs at the back of his neck stood on end. The house was quiet. Too quiet. He ran from room to room yelling her name, and was halfway up the stairs when

Dot appeared on the landing with a frown. "Lord almighty. Why are you shouting?"

Ransom grabbed her roughly by the shoulders and Dot's breath caught, eyes round. "Where's Clare?"

"In the woods," she stammered. "She went in by the trail. What's happened? I told her to watch the time."

He willed himself to stay calm. "There's a black SUV rental parked at the end of your driveway. The men driving it are murderers."

"Murderers!" Dot gasped. She looked to the woods and her face paled.

"Call the police," Ransom ordered, thundering down the stairs. He hit the trail at a dead run.

d

With the gorge to Clare's back, retreat was impossible. Stuffing her trembling hands into her coat pockets, she lifted her chin and stared at the men, refusing to show fear. "What do you want?"

The white-haired man regarded her with steely eyes and said nothing, his bulging muscles evident even under his jacket.

The bearded man calmly lit a cigarette. Taking a long drag, he exhaled the smoke from his nose like a dragon. "Our employer is offering you the opportunity to work for his company," he said. "The position is vice president in charge of new accounts."

Clare shook her head, trying to clear the cobwebs. "You're offering me a job?"

"An opportunity," he corrected. "The base salary is two hundred fifty thousand."

"Dollars?" Clare croaked

"Plus full health benefits, three weeks paid vacation,

and a percentage for every new account you bring in." Reaching inside his jacket, he pulled out a white envelope and handed it to her. "Signing bonus," he explained.

Clare peered inside the envelope at a five thousand dollar cashier's check with her name on it. She gulped. Could this be happening to her? Even without the added incentives, the beginning wage was more than ten times the amount the store had paid her. With that kind of money, she could pay off her loans and save for a business of her own.

For a brief moment Clare forgot she was standing perilously close to the edge of a rocky gorge, a couple slippery steps from what would be certain death. In this moment, all was sugarplums and happy possibilities.

Toeing out the cigarette, the bearded man's hard, dark eyes assessed her. "We have a deal, then?"

As Clare stared at the man, an instinctive distrust kicked in. "I'm sorry, I don't want to sound ungrateful, but who's your employer? It seems odd to make such a generous offer without an interview."

He gave a vague shrug. "Mr. Renwalt's methods are his own. He asked us to talk to you for him."

"Renwalt?" Clare's eyes narrowed. "As in Nicholas Renwalt of Renwalt Industries? *That's* who wants to hire me? The man is nothing more than a tyrant, enslaving women and children to sew his clothes."

Irritation crossed the bearded man's face. "A matter of opinion," he said stiffly.

"It's the opinion of our country's labor laws. Not to mention exposing his employees to deadly chemicals. Wherever he builds a factory, the community's cancer rate skyrockets."

He dismissed Clare's accusation with a wave of his hand. "Mr. Renwalt employs thousands who otherwise wouldn't have anything."

"Money is all Nicholas Renwalt cares about," Clare said. "He's turned his back on people and the planet, and won't take responsibility for his decisions." She tore the check in two and flung it. "I'd never work for him."

Taking a step to leave, the blond man moved forward, blocking her way. With as much courage as she could muster, she squared her shoulders and glared at the man, more than aware he was a foot taller and twice her weight. "Get out of my way," she ordered, proud of the fact there was only a slight tremor in her voice.

Not the least intimidated, the hulking blond peered at Clare with the chilling warmth of a cobra and took another step forward, crowding her closer to the edge. Pushing him aside would be like pushing aside a mountain.

Panic seized her as warning bells clamored inside her head. The whole situation was surreal. *It's okay, go around him,* she told herself. But when she tried to sidestep past him, he snared her hand in a vice-like grip. Jerking her back hard, her shoulder popped from its socket.

She cried out as searing pain blazed down her arm to her fingertips. Tears sprang to her eyes. With a firm hold on Clare's wrist, the man leaned her far over the ledge. Her feet scrambled for a toehold. Loose stones and ice fell a hundred feet into the gorge below.

Clare's heart hammered wildly inside her chest as she frantically clutched at the man with her free hand, catching hold of his sleeve. Looking into his hard gray eyes, her blood ran cold with the realization he'd think no more of ending her life than he would a pesky gnat.

The bearded man calmly stepped to the ledge and looked over the side. "Long way down," he observed.

"Why are you doing this?" she asked.

Straightening, he looked at Clare with grim satisfaction. Even as she fought back tears, his smugness maddened her to no end. "Mr. Renwalt doesn't care for the way you've been smearing his good name," he said. "Your petition to keep his products out of stores has caused him worry. Thanks to your meddling, several of his largest customers canceled their orders." He leaned toward her, close enough for Clare to smell the cigarettes on his breath. "Since you refused Mr. Renwalt's generosity, there's another way you can remedy the situation. Withdraw your petition and sign a brief statement prepared by Mr. Renwalt. You'll be compensated for your time."

"Let me guess. The statement makes me out as a liar."

Anger flared in his dark eyes. "Be smart. Take the money and withdraw your petition."

"Or what?" she asked.

His look turned menacing. "It's icy. You might slip."

Clare closed her eyes and let the tears roll. The pain in her shoulder was nearly unbearable. If only she hadn't gone on this walk. She should've listened to Ransom and stayed inside. God, how she wished he were with her.

She tried to think what he would do, and a thought popped into her mind as if someone had whispered it to her: *Everything in your life is a great gift or it would not be there. Do not reject your gifts.*

The thought was so radical that her eyes flew open.

She peered into the dull, remorseless eyes of the man she clung to. He'd drop her without thinking twice. This man was a cold-hearted killer. How could *he* be a gift?

Do not judge, the quiet, yet persistent voice told her. *There are no villains, only misguided, hurting people. You are for one another like mirrors and will reflect every thought and every feeling you have about who you are. Therefore, you are each other's helpers in disguise.*

Clare heard the voice in her mind as if it was her own, although never before had she had such thoughts. What did it mean? Was it possible she was this man's mirror? What was she showing him? Hate? Anger? Fear?

Do not fear what you've created, the voice said. *Right or wrong action springs from motivation. Let Love be your motivation. See as God sees.*

See as God sees, Clare silently repeated to herself. She took a deep calming breath as Ransom had taught her. From the crown of her head to her toes, tingling energy hummed through her body, heightening within her a powerful sense of well-being. Suddenly, she wasn't so afraid anymore. She wasn't alone. God was with her.

She inhaled again, deepening the connection, feeling the pulse lift her vibration higher. Ransom's words came back to her: *You can only give from what you have.*

What did she have to give?

Everything you need is within you, the voice answered. *The world is a huge gift-making machine. Love, peace, and joy are present in every circumstance and available to all. Stay present. What you choose in this moment signifies the path you intend to take in your im-*

mediate future. Choose your path without fear.

Determined to see as God sees, Clare cleared her mind of thought, took her eyes slightly out of focus, and concentrated on her captor with feelings of compassion. A new understanding came to her. No one would consciously treat another in this way if they were not in tremendous pain.

Clare knew about pain. She wouldn't wish the oppressive self-loathing she'd carried on her worst enemy. If he felt even half the torturous weight she did, he'd suffered enough. She began to feel sorry for him and had no desire to add to his suffering.

At that thought, a whoosh of warmth rushed into her heart. Her breath caught as she saw a golden halo of shimmering light around the man.

Glancing at their tightly clasped hands bathed in the same golden light, they took on a transparent quality. Clare could barely tell where her fingers ended and his began. The light emanated from within him, brightly illuminating his hair, his skin, his face.

She watched him blink in slow motion, and saw the dark shield lift from his eyes and give way to sparkling warmth in much the same way a window shade opens to let in sunlight. The transformation was miraculous. When he looked at her, he saw her. Not some random stranger, but *her.*

The sound of a match being struck drew Clare's attention. The bearded man lit another cigarette. The smoke curled from his mouth into the frigid air. "Well, what's it going to be?" he asked her.

Clare turned to the blond man. "Do you want to hurt me?"

The big guy wavered with uncertainty. He looked to the bearded man for direction. "I don't think she's going to sign anything," he said.

The bearded man's nostrils flared. He flicked the cigarette over the ledge. "Stupid bitch," he spat, and signaled for his partner to let her go.

The blond hesitated. He looked at Clare with troubled eyes. Sweat beaded his forehead as he struggled to hang onto her.

With her heart in her throat, Clare held his eyes and prayed: *Please give us both the courage to listen with our hearts and see one another as God sees us.*

A rock let loose and Clare's footing slipped. She screamed, and his grip tightened around her wrist.

"What are you waiting for?" the bearded man asked gruffly. "Let go."

The blond man couldn't let go. His mouth pressed into a hard line, and his muscles strained as he pulled Clare onto solid ground.

Enraged with disbelief, the bearded man rushed forward and shoved Clare over the ledge. There was a cold wind at her back as she fell, but she wasn't afraid. An unfamiliar silence had captured her attention. She could hear things in a way she couldn't before. It was as if a low background static she hadn't known existed was now gone.

She closed her eyes. A crow cawed overhead, the voice full and round and so indescribably lovely she could listen to this one sound for an eternity.

Below her, deep in the icy water, a trout navigated the current. The trail he cut sounded like tinkling piano keys. How had she not heard this music before?

So this is what it felt like to die. Peaceful and unhurried, as if she had nothing but time. Adam popped into her mind. She saw him sitting on the side of his bed, a picture of her in his hands. There was longing in him she hadn't imagined. He ached for her. *Ached.*

She felt a click in her heart, like a door opening. Every regret and pent-up emotion within her dissolved. Never had she been this light, this free. Overwhelmed with love and gratitude for everyone and every circumstance, she knew the purpose of life. Life was for her. The good, the bad, the indifferent were gifts wrapped in miracles waiting for her to determine how best to use them.

A prayer flashed in her mind. *Thank you for my life. It's perfect.*

Whoosh! The air was forced from Clare's lungs when she landed, and she struggled mightily for that first breath. Mercifully, there wasn't any pain. When she opened her eyes, she found herself securely cradled in Ransom's strong arms. His skin had become almost translucent with the loving light deep within him. Clare stared into those sparkling green eyes, and his face lit with a grin. "Gotcha."

Epilogue

TRAFFIC was light as Clare turned off the freeway and drove her Camry west toward France Avenue, an area in the Twin Cities known for trendy boutiques, gourmet restaurants, and stately homes. Clare was dressed in an old sweatshirt and jeans, and her car was packed with gallons of paint and supplies. A stepladder was angled over the seats. Strapped next to her in the passenger seat, was a lush, three-foot tall plant with glistening leaves.

At a stoplight, Clare stuck a finger inside the pot testing for moisture. Hard to believe this healthy plant had been on death's door four months earlier. It had come a long way in those few months and, admittedly, she had too.

Four months, she mused. That's how long it had been since Ransom rescued her at the bottom of the ravine. Every detail of that moment was etched on her heart. It was the last time she saw him, though she knew he was always with her. Mostly he sent her pennies, or messed with her lights, or gave her goosebumps so she'd know he was around protecting her, guiding her, giving her hope. Knowing she wasn't alone brought her an unshakable sense of peace.

No longer afraid, Clare trusted her instincts and worked to raise her vibration. The driving force that formed planets and turned winter to spring was alive and operating inside her as well. Although she had no control over the 'how' of life, and for this she was grateful, she came to understand that through intention she could direct her tiny perception of this great force, and found it moved perfectly and automatically in the creation of her reality.

Clare discovered that the higher her energy, the clearer her inner messages, and the easier it became for her to act on them. She also learned when not to pursue a course of action by how she felt. If it was a struggle with every door closing, she stopped whatever she was trying to do and waited in alert silence for God's direction, as Ransom had taught her. When she let Life create through her without judging how something had to be, she found the universe provided everything she needed with ease.

And what had Life and she co-created? The cutest shop on the planet! Or it would be after she gave the walls a fresh coat of paint and filled the space with her line of clothing.

Everything had come together so fast. Stephen, her co-worker at the department store, had called her a month earlier excited with news. One of his regular customers mentioned needing a renter for a small store with lots of potential. Did he know anyone who might be interested? Of course he thought of Clare!

When Clare saw the red brick building for the first time, her heart skipped a beat. It had a massive oak door, striped awnings, and huge front windows with window boxes perfect for red geraniums and trailing ivy. Immediately she saw her clothing displayed in those windows. And how cool would her sign look hanging above that great old door?

When she stepped inside and saw the wood plank flooring and spiral staircase leading to a loft, her legs got rubbery. The loft, she knew, would make a perfect office. And when she pushed through a door and found herself in a separate back room large enough for a cutting table and her sewing machines, she nearly collapsed into a puddle of drooling lust. The final clincher had been the vintage dressmaker's form she'd found in a storeroom closet. It was a sign. She *had* to have this building.

Filled with hope, she was surprised to learn the rent was more than she could afford. But instead of letting herself be disappointed like she used to, she maintained a high vibration and visualized the greatest good for every person who walked into this space to buy her clothes. Moments later, the owner decided to rent to her anyway, only charging a percentage of what she earned.

Her dream was becoming reality. She didn't think she could be any happier until she saw Adam waiting against her building. Dressed as she was in painting clothes, he had a hand wrapped around an extension roller. He never looked more handsome.

She parked at the curb, and Adam opened her door.

"Been waiting long?" she asked him.

"Yes," he said pulling her into him.

He kissed her long and hard, and she didn't care in the least that they were standing on a busy street with people staring at them. Finally he let her go, and immediately Clare missed his lips on hers. Painting didn't seem like such a great idea anymore.

Adam must have had the same thought, because he let out some air as he reluctantly stepped back from her. "Uh, I guess we'd better get to work," he said.

Grabbing the ladder from the car, he headed for the

building. Clare let out a sigh of her own and unbuckled the plant. She gave it a warning look. "I trust you to keep me from throwing myself at that gorgeous man. Brace yourself. It's going to be a huge challenge."

Confident that at least the plant had everything under control, she wrestled it from the car and marched to the door. Adam smiled at her as she struggled with the lock.

"Here, let me," he said. Turning the key, he pushed the door open and ushered her inside.

Clare set the plant in the front window and was about to go back to the car for paint when Adam called her over.

"Look what I found on the floor," he said. Pressing a penny into her hand, his voice turned husky as he drew her closer. "This must be your lucky day, Clare Davis."

Fisting Adam's sweatshirt, Clare pulled him into a kiss. Ransom told her to live in the present. She could paint these walls tomorrow.

Dear Reader,

Thank you for reading GUARDING CLARE. If you enjoyed this book, please consider leaving a rating and review. Your comments really help new books get noticed, and every review is greatly appreciated.

If you want to stay in touch, I'd love to hear from you! Here's how you can connect with me:

Email: marymbauer.author@gmail.com

Facebook:
https://www.facebook.com/marymbauer.author/

Website: www.marymbauer.com

With love for your journey,
Mary